"We need someone to cover us." More shots shattered the air and Ryder pushed Emma down again, his breath coming in huffs.

He looked at the trees again, then pulled out his cell and sent an alert text to all available personnel.

Ryder glanced toward the barn and saw rifles peeking out of windows and doors. Then he moved his head slightly toward the house. A curtain was pulled back in an upstairs window.

Lowering his head, he ignored the floral scent wafting from Emma's hair and whispered in her ear. "When I say go, I want you to run toward the barn, toward the doors. Someone will let you inside."

"What about you?"

"I'm going to cover you, along with my men inside who are waiting."

"Are you sure this will work?"

"If you run fast, yes." He looked into her eyes, his heart beating against hers. "Belly-crawl if you have to and don't look back."

She nodded and gave him a solid stare. "Be careful, Ryder."

Another shot hit the air.

"Just do it, Emma."

With over seventy books published and millions in print, **Lenora Worth** writes award-winning romance and romantic suspense. Three of her books finaled in the ACFW Carol Awards, and her Love Inspired Suspense novel *Body of Evidence* became a *New York Times* bestseller. Her novella in *Mistletoe Kisses* made her a *USA TODAY* bestselling author. Lenora goes on adventures with her retired husband, Don, and enjoys reading, baking and shopping... especially shoe shopping.

Books by Lenora Worth

Love Inspired Suspense

Undercover Memories

Military K-9 Unit

Rescue Operation

Classified K-9 Unit

Tracker
Classified K-9 Unit Christmas
"A Killer Christmas"

Rookie K-9 Unit

Truth and Consequences
Rookie K-9 Unit Christmas
"Holiday High Alert"

Visit the Author Profile page at Harlequin.com for more titles.

UNDERCOVER MEMORIES

LENORA WORTH

HARLEQUIN® LOVE INSPIRED® SUSPENSE

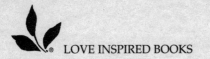

LOVE INSPIRED BOOKS

Recycling programs for this product may not exist in your area.

ISBN-13: 978-1-335-49065-0

Undercover Memories

Copyright © 2018 by Lenora H. Nazworth

www.Harlequin.com

Printed in U.S.A.

In the fear of the Lord is strong confidence: and his children shall have a place of refuge.
–Proverbs 14:26

In memory of all the children who don't find their way home. You are not forgotten.

ONE

Detective Ryder Palladin listened to the grit and static of the scanner and hit a fist against the steering wheel of the rusty, old undercover vehicle. He was hot and tired and full of bad coffee. "Daughtry, come in."

He'd been sitting in this broken-up, weed-infested parking lot in the armpit of downtown Dallas for the better part of an hour, waiting to see if Daughtry could get their man. Petey Smith was low on the ladder to drug lord success, a gofer really. And as squirrely as a back-alley rodent. He'd squeal before they slammed the bars on his jail cell.

If Daughtry ever signaled that he had him.

His younger, overly confident partner's voice finally came through on Ryder's earbud. "What's the matter, cowboy? Miss me?"

"Just report," Ryder growled back, ready to get home. His partner, Pierce Daughtry, had joined Vice two years ago when the man had been extremely wet behind the ears. Sometimes, Ryder believed Pierce was still a rookie, but the kid had proved himself over and over. He'd better come through tonight. Ryder wanted to finish this shift and head to his Fort Worth ranch for the weekend.

"Did you find Petey?"

"Nope, but I found a situation," Pierce replied in his

laid-back Texas drawl. "Might want to come and take a look at this one."

"I sent you in to surveil one shady criminal."

"I'm not kidding, man," Pierce replied. "I… I think I've found a dead woman."

"Call 911."

Ryder let up with the chitchat and got out of the unmarked car at a run, his semiautomatic pistol drawn, his cowboy boots hitting the ragged sidewalk tearing through one of the worst areas of downtown. A Texas-size summer heat sizzled all around him as his breath cut through the heavy humidity and the dank smells of rotting garbage and worse.

Rounding a dark corner, he saw Pierce Daughtry up ahead in the alley, bent over what could only be the discovery he'd made.

"She's still alive, but barely," Pierce said on a loud whisper while Ryder stared down at the still figure. "I think I interrupted them. That big bouncer and his scrawny sidekick."

"Did you try to stop them?"

Pierce did an eye roll. "What, and give away my cover?"

Ryder did a return eye roll. "What happened?"

"They saw me coming around the corner and turned and ran in the other direction," he said with a grim grin. "I gave chase but they got away before I could do anything much. Took off in a black truck." Shrugging, he added with dripping sarcasm, "And that's when I *reported* to you, Oh-Great-One."

"They left her for dead," Ryder finished, ignoring the sarcasm since it kept them both grounded. "I'll check her for ID."

Ryder bent down over the woman and immediately noticed the dark blob of blood on the left side of her head just above her temple. Shining a penlight, he took in her face. Pretty in an intriguing, freckled way. Wearing just enough lipstick to make him wonder. From what he could tell from the sickly yellow streetlight hanging by a thread in the corner, dark auburn-colored hair, long and matted with blood, a slender, buff body, average size in height. She wore jeans and a lightweight blue button-up shirt. And a nice pair of black boots. Pointed toes that looked lethal.

Sirens sounded off in the distance.

"Hang on, beautiful," he said after checking for a pulse. Weak, but still fighting. Careful, he frisked her, searching for identification. He found a tiny wallet in her back jeans pocket, along with a credit card and some cash, which indicated whoever did this wasn't trying to rob her. But Pierce showing up could have stopped that. He did say they'd run away.

Careful, Ryder searched her once more and found two more interesting items.

A Glock semiautomatic nestled against her backbone. He held the gun with the handkerchief he kept in his coat pocket and then handed it off to Pierce for safekeeping. Then he went back to the wallet to see if he could find any names or meeting schedules. This was interesting— her wallet also contained a private investigator's license.

Emma Langston. From what he could see from the yellow glow of the streetlight, the photo matched her physical appearance. Birth date matched the age she looked to be—around thirty-one years old. Her driver's license was registered to Galveston County and her address listed a property in Galveston. She'd sure come a long way inland for something.

Or someone. Who was this unconscious beauty after?

"Must be important for you to case this joint," he mumbled while he checked her pulse and tried to make her comfortable. Staring down at her, he asked, "What's the story, Red?"

Ryder silently prayed she would wake up and answer that question. And all of the other ones forming in his head, too.

Pain stomped through her head like a herd of longhorns.

Trying to push through, she rode the wave of urgency sounding like an alarm throughout her system.

Emma woke with a start, sweat chilling her body and a muted sun shining through the slanted blinds. Sunrise or sunset? Glancing around, she blinked and went into defense mode. She was in a hospital room. "Hey?"

That set off all kinds of alarm bells, but then another kind of panic set in. The kind that could make a person nauseated and full of sick dread. Emma didn't like this feeling of floating on an empty cloud while her head screamed with agony.

What had happened to her?

She blinked and gripped the sheets, her gaze moving to the beeping machines hooked up to her body. She hated needles. But when she lifted her head, it rolled like a punching bag. A ragged pain shot through her, cutting off her breath.

The panic thickened like a heavy fog.

She couldn't *remember* what had happened to her, but her whole body ached in a crushing sequence that moved from her brain to her toes.

"Hey?" she called again and then after a frantic search for the bed's remote control handle, she buzzed for a nurse.

And got one right away. "Tell Dr. Sherrington she's awake. And…keep that detective out of here until we can check her vitals and verify her condition."

Detective?

Emma watched as the nurse did her thing. Blood pressure, heart rate, beep, beep. Lifting tubes and checking fluid bags. Beep, beep, beep. Emma touched her head because at least a hundred hammers kept knocking at her brain. Heavy bandages. "What happened to me?"

The nurse shined a light into her eyes. "You suffered a concussion."

"How?"

The nurse summed her up and, from the look of respect in her eyes, must have decided Emma could handle the truth. "Blunt force object. Otherwise called a baseball bat." Then the nurse checked her blood pressure. "But you were smart. Looks like you fought back and possibly deflected the blow, according to the paramedics who brought you in last night."

Emma had a flash of memory, a feeling of bracing against something. And the one last thought. *This is gonna hurt.*

But she forced control. "Oh, okay. Happens a lot."

She didn't know why she'd said that or how she even knew that she'd been injured before. And that scared her more than knowing.

The gray-haired doctor came in, his dour expression not really helping. "You've been through quite an ordeal, haven't you?"

Emma didn't tolerate patronizing. "Well, I don't know. I can't quite remember."

She pushed at the panic following that statement. She wouldn't give anyone the satisfaction of watching her cave. Trying to breathe in and out, in and out, she watched the doctor watching her.

He checked her over, poking and prodding and testing. Moving his bright light and his fingers in front of her eyes, asking if she could feel this or see that. She didn't want to feel anything, but she did want to see it all in her mind.

"Things are fuzzy," she admitted, hoping he'd fill in the blanks.

Finally, he looked at her chart and then he looked at her. "What do you remember?"

She shook her head, swallowed the fear. She could go dark and not discuss this. That MO had worked for her for years now.

And how had she remembered *that*?

"Talk to me," the doctor said, no longer in a playful mood. "We need to get you well."

Emma nodded and decided it might be wise to cooperate. "Doc, I... I don't remember anything much."

"Do you know your name?"

She blinked, thought long enough to make the hammers go into overtime. "Emma?"

"Yes, you're Emma Langston. That's a start." He gave her chart to the nurse. "Give it some time. We'll do more tests and see how you progress. You've suffered a moderate but serious concussion, but you woke up within the one- to twenty-four-hour period, and that's a plus. No swelling or bleeding on the brain. Another good thing. Temporary amnesia is common after a head injury, but we'll monitor you while we wait it out."

"I don't have time to wait it out," she replied, trying to get out of the bed. She knew one thing: she had to be somewhere. But where and why?

The doctor pushed her back down. "Whoa, you can't go anywhere just yet. You've been unconscious for close to fifteen hours now." Showing an edge of compassion, he added, "You'll need some therapy. Head trauma is serious stuff."

"I'll be okay," Emma said, already dizzy again. "I've been here that long?"

The doctor nodded. "They brought you in around midnight and now it's five in the afternoon."

"That's long enough for me."

"Let me be the judge of that."

He asked some more questions. She gave feeble, weak answers. She couldn't bluff her way out of this one.

Why am I here?

"Where am I?" she finally asked, wishing she could remember. "What city is this?"

He named the hospital. "You're in Dallas, Texas. Do you remember where you came from?"

Shards of memories danced just out of her reach.

Dear Lord, help me. Help me in my time of need.

Funny, she remembered praying that same prayer long ago. For some reason, Emma wanted to cry. To curl up and cry, long and hard. But she didn't cry, she reminded herself. That much she knew.

"That's a loaded question," she retorted, pushing away the lump in her throat. "But right now, I can't answer it."

Emma had to get out of this hospital. She'd come to Dallas for a reason, obviously. But…she couldn't remember what she was doing here.

Then she did remember something. Grabbing the nurse's arm, she said, "You mentioned a detective. What's he got to do with this?"

"He's been waiting most of the day to talk to you," the nurse replied. "I can send him away."

"No. Send him in," Emma said. "Maybe he can help me piece things together."

The nurse looked skeptical but finally nodded. "I'll ask Dr. Sherrington."

"No. I said let me speak to the detective. Now."

"I'll go and find him," the nurse responded.

Emma sank back against the pillow, drowsiness tugging at her consciousness. She had to talk to that detective. Had she done something wrong? Or did he know who'd done this to her?

She waited, holding her breath, her prayers as scattered as her memories. The detective might be the one person who could tell her why she had such a strong urgency in her heart to get out of here.

He flashed his badge. "Detective Ryder Palladin."

Emma stared up at the man standing at the foot of her hospital bed. He filled the room and made it shrink until she felt his too-close appraisal.

To mask her fears and confusion, she turned things back toward him. "Palladin? Really?"

His wry grin told her he got that a lot.

"Yep. It's my real name. But with two Ls."

"Like the cellular palladin, not the gunslinger Paladin?"

"So we've established you know your chemistry and that you remember that old Western series."

Surprised at herself, she nodded, a memory of sitting on a sofa with some other children when she was tiny hitting her in the gut with a sweet intensity. Did she have a family somewhere? "I guess so. The doc told me I'd have little clusters of memories. Islands of memories, he called them."

Ryder Palladin didn't look like a big-city detective. More like a cowboy straight out of *that* old Western. Complete with a cream-colored hat, plaid button-up shirt and nicely worn jeans. With dark longish wavy hair and glinting bronze-brown eyes that held a gold mine of secrets.

He took off his hat and allowed her to enjoy all that luscious wavy hair. "Do you remember who you are?"

"Emma. Emma Langston, according to the doctor."

"But not according to you?"

"I'm remembering bits and pieces. Why are you here?"

Lifting a dark slanted brow, he chuckled while his secretive gaze did a round on her. "You get right to the heart of things, don't you?"

"I don't have time for idle chatter."

He absorbed that with classic detective disdain. "Need to be somewhere in a hurry, Emma Langston?"

She didn't like his smug attitude or the way he made tiny little shivering sensations float down her spine. "What do you know about me?"

"I'm the one who asks the questions," he retorted, throwing his hat in a nearby chair. He had the kind of hair a woman wanted to grab onto and hold. Silky, shining, unruly.

"I'm the one who needs to know what happened," she replied, her head hammering and grinding in pain while her heart jumped in a fast-beating tempo.

"You got hit with a baseball bat."

He watched her cringe. "Yeah, the nurse told me. But I think I can almost remember that. I need a few more details."

He put his hands against the foot of the bed. His big, tanned hands. "You were at the Blue Bull Bar—the Triple B to the locals. Do you almost remember that, too?"

Emma swallowed away the terror of not remembering, of not knowing. She liked to be in control—of her emotions, of her life, of her work. Somehow, she did know *that*.

"Why would I go there?"

He gave her that lazy slide of a gaze again. "*I'm* asking you."

"*I* don't remember."

"Your ID shows you're a private investigator from Galveston."

Emma inhaled a breath, the sound of ocean waves crashing against a seawall filling her mind. Images of a tiny beach house, all blue and white and sunny, made her feel secure. But other memories of fear and urgency seemed to want to darken her mind.

He picked up on her confusion right away. "Do you remember that now?"

"Some. Maybe. I can see the beach in my mind. A house. I might live there. But why did I come to Dallas?"

"I'm thinking you were at the Triple B looking for someone or maybe tailing someone."

"Why were you there?"

"Do you always answer a question with a question?"

"I don't know. I can't remember."

That retort won her a grin of appreciation. "And she has a wicked sense of humor at that."

"Seriously, why were you there? It might help me remember."

"Good try." He eyed her for a long minute, still not quite trusting her. Then he leaned in. "I work Vice."

"A vice detective? Did I do something wrong?"

"No. But my partner found you unconscious in the alley behind the Triple B."

Another memory of walking into a seedy, dark bar, the smell of beer and smoke assaulting her, making her feel sick. Stares and whispers and…questions.

"I asked some questions."

"I reckon you did."

"They told me to get out."

"I reckon they would."

"I can't remember why I went there." The panic started up. "I need to get out of here and find out what's going on." She lifted, tried to sit up. But her head went wild with pain and agony, causing her to turn dizzy and confused.

"Hey, hey," he said, his hand on her arm strong and steady, his eyes kind now. "Lie back. You can't go anywhere just yet."

Emma gulped in air, nodded. Pretended she hadn't noticed his touch. Crazy that this man seemed to hit all the marks even when she was in crisis mode. Even when she couldn't remember if she was married or single. Single sounded more like it. Something she did need to remember. "Do you know who did this to me?"

He pulled out two grainy snapshots that made her have a flash of a memory. She'd taken such shots in her line of work.

"Do you recognize these two men?"

Emma squinted against the pain in her head and carefully studied both photos. "I don't know. The skinny one seems familiar."

He nodded and put the pictures back in his shirt pocket.

"Can I get you anything?" he asked, his tiger eyes full of concern.

"My mind back."

"We're working on that."

"And you look so happy about it," she noted out loud.

He stood, his gaze holding hers for a beat too long. "Big Sam and Little Eddie guard that place. We call them a bounce and an ounce. One's big, bald and beefy—"

"—And the other's short, scrawny and scared?"

"Good description."

"He came at me—the little one." She motioned to his pocket. "That could be the same two men—in the photo. The skinny one came at me while the big one made sure I couldn't get away. And I told myself it would hurt. I tried to fight, get to a weapon."

"I know," the detective said. "You're alive because you fought, and that's amazing." Then he shifted, crossed his big arms over his chest. "If my partner hadn't come along, you might be dead. He scared them away."

"He saw them?"

"He thinks it was them but he can't be sure. Okay, we know it was them but…we need your take on that. Identifying them can help." He studied her for a couple of beats. "We did find traces of epidermis underneath your nails. Waiting on the DNA from that and the other bits and pieces of evidence we collected."

Emma had a flash, a memory of her fingernails digging into skin. "I need to get out of here."

"Why?"

"I don't know. I have to figure this out."

"Rest," he said, his tone gentle now, his eyes washed in empathy. "Let me do the figuring."

Confused and wishing she didn't have to depend on him, Emma gave him an astonished stare. "You'll do that for me?"

Those eyes gazed at her with all the intensity of a strobe light. "You're a victim of a crime and it happened on my watch, so yeah, I'll do that for you."

"You didn't tell me why *you* were there."

"I like the neighborhood."

With that, he handed her his card. "Call me if you remember anything else. Anything at all."

Emma watched him go, her eyes traveling down to his feet, her heart excited to take the ride with her.

Yep. Boots. Buttery tan and worn but probably handmade.

She wanted to ask how a cowboy like him had wound up working Vice in the first place.

She'd get to that question next time she saw him.

Because she knew the good-looking detective would be back.

He'd want answers. Well, she wanted answers, too.
They had that much in common already.

TWO

The next day, Ryder headed back to the hospital to check on Emma. He'd put a patrol on her door while he did some digging on both the pretty PI with the head wound and the two goons who'd allegedly left her for dead.

One perk of being a vice cop, if there was such a thing. He had a lot of confidential informants who'd squeal for anything from money to food to opioids to get them through the day. He didn't hand out drugs as prizes, but he did offer people cash to get food or do whatever their conscience allowed or forced them to do. Some of his informants had turned their lives around and often thanked Ryder for helping them. Some died or disappeared.

But last night, one had come through for him.

"I saw her," the kid everyone called Junior had told him in a hushed voice while they hid behind some buildings and trees about a block from the Triple B. His eyes were swollen from too much vodka and pot and his face showed signs of a whole lot of soul-searching and street-walking. "She was pretty. Stood out. Asked a lot of questions. Wanted to know if any underage teens hung out at the Triple B."

"Underage teens? So you think she was looking for someone? A runaway maybe?"

"Maybe. I told her all kinds come and go and she mentioned a name, but then I got out of there when Bounce and Ounce started stalking her."

Ryder showed the CI a grainy picture of Emma he'd pulled from a social media page. "Does this look like the woman you saw?"

"Yep. I think that's her. I remember that shiny hair—like red wine. She looked tough."

"Yeah." Ryder could attest to that and the shiny auburn hair. "Do you remember the name she mentioned?"

"No. Like I said, I had to leave quick."

So now Ryder had established she had been in the bar and why she might have been there. And he had a possible eyewitness to seeing Bounce and Ounce going after her. But he knew from past experience the kid wouldn't go on record with this information.

He'd given the kid a twenty. "Go get a shower and some food at the shelter down the street."

Ryder figured the kid would buy drugs and liquor with the money but prayed he'd at least get some food in him. Nasty business, the things Ryder saw each day. But he always remembered his daddy's advice.

"Pray the ugly away."

I'm trying, Daddy.

Remembering his larger-than-life father who'd been sheriff in Denton County for twenty-eight years before he'd been shot down while off duty, Ryder again wondered why he did this job. He'd just gone off to college when his dad had died. Ryder had come home and finished up at a junior college near the ranch. Criminal justice. Then he'd headed to the police academy and never looked back. Or maybe he always looked back. Hard to tell.

He wanted justice, of course. He could go home to the ranch that had been in his family for generations and make a nice living off the livestock and the land, but this job kept tugging him back. According to his mother, he had a death wish. One she and his teenaged sister wanted him to give up.

Ryder wasn't quite ready to walk away from crime.

Especially not now. Emma Langston had put a kink in his undercover investigation, but she'd also rallied some long-lost thread of feeling inside his heart. Curiosity had him by the throat. Her expressive eyes had him by the heart.

Not wise. No time for such notions. He didn't take the time to have a love life. His job scared women away. His mother tried to set him up with fine, upstanding church-going single women. But the minute he mentioned working Vice in downtown Dallas, he never saw those sweet women again and usually saw wedding photos of them on social media. That kind married doctors and lawyers and ranchers. Not detectives who walked through the seamy, ugly side of life. Nope. No time to even think about Emma's immediate hold on him.

She's not that kind.

Okay, his always-arguing brain had him on that one.

She was not that kind at all. Different. Tough. Determined. Strong. Afraid. Secretive. Reckless and ruthless.

Maybe he didn't need her kind in his life either.

But he checked with the nurses' station and got permission to go in and see Emma even while his brain told him to let it go. Then he talked to the officer who'd stood watch.

"All quiet," Seth Conyers said. "I sat in that chair all night and I have the bad back to prove it."

"I'll be here for a while," Ryder told the officer. "Go on home to your wife. I'll stay until your relief shows up."

Ryder didn't want to be at the station right now anyway.

As he'd figured, Bobby Doug Manchester had shown up to speak to the chief about "the constant barrage of criminals and indecent people who walked the streets of Dallas." Ryder had left with the echo of the pompous businessman's sarcastic wrath ringing in his ears.

"You keep at it, Detective Palladin. You're doing such a great job."

Ryder knocked and heard Emma call out, "Come in."

She sat up in bed, her blue-green eyes watching the door with an alertness he recognized all too well as a flight risk. But her color was back and, other than a few bruises and the bandage on one side of her head, she looked much better.

Lifting her chin, she asked, "Did you send the uniform away?"

"You mean Seth? Yeah, he was ready for some shut-eye."

"Are you his replacement?"

"And good morning to you, too."

"I need your help to get me out of here."

"Why, yes, I had a pretty good night myself, and thank you for asking."

She sank back, her long hair slinking over her shoulder. "Sorry. I don't make a good patient."

"I never would have guessed."

"I'm starving."

"Didn't they feed you?"

"I didn't like the food here."

"That explains why you're still hungry. Or maybe just *hangry*."

"I'm bored and aggravated—and hungry and angry. Will you help me?"

Letting out a tired sigh, Ryder sat down in the high-backed recliner across from the bed. "What exactly do you want me to do? Smuggle in some real food?"

"Bust me out of here," she said on a quiet note that kind of tugged at his heartstrings. "I could use a good hamburger."

Even with a huge bandage on her head, the woman showed a strength that seemed to buzz with electricity. That or he'd had one too many cups of coffee this morning. Ryder had never met anyone quite like Emma Langston. Here she sat with a busted head and wearing a faded hospital gown, but she had more gumption and grit than most of the notorious criminals he came up against on a daily basis. And she sure looked a whole lot prettier than them, too.

But he could not indulge in all that gumption and grit and prettiness. This job demanded all of his attention. He had to get to the bottom of why she was here so he could get on with his own investigation.

"I'm pretty sure your doctor and my chief would both frown on that," he replied, referring to her earlier question.

"And I'm pretty sure you're the kind who doesn't worry about being frowned upon."

"You know me so well already?"

"I know your kind."

Glancing around, he took in that assumption and said, "So did you remember anything else?"

"I didn't sleep, so I had time to think about things."

That wasn't exactly a good answer. "And?"

"And I need to be out there, not lying here."

"You do know you have a head injury even if your head is too hard to get that, right? What does your doctor say?"

"He's done a set of questions and because I can't answer all of them, he wants me to rest. But I can't rest."

"What did you remember, Emma? And don't try to con me."

* * *

Emma worried with her covers, her fingers curling into the soft white fleece of the warm blanket. How much could she trust him? How much did he know already? What if he was part of this? What if he knew more than he was letting on?

Testing him, she asked, "How far did you get with my background check?"

His eyebrows winged up in surprise. "Far enough. Since you either can't or won't share what you remember, I'll tell you what I know."

She didn't move. Couldn't move. Fighting with her brain all night had brought her nothing but a bad case of anxiety. Even her dreams made no sense.

"You were born in Galveston. You attended school there and in Houston—several different schools—but you were a straight-A student. Graduated with honors and a little scholarship money and went to the University of Texas. Studied criminology. Worked as a police officer for two years and then ventured out on your own to become a private investigator."

He named her address, and a vague memory came alive inside her brain. A memory of almost being at peace with herself.

Almost.

"I was a police officer?" Emma squinted, tried to find the shattered pieces of her memory. Faces and arguments, shame and danger. She didn't want to remember.

Those scattered memories, just as the doctor had said. But the doctor had also told her that happened in about a third of amnesia patients. Emma thought these little islands of floating memories made it much worse. They offered glimmers of hope but made her head feel like a jigsaw puzzle.

Ryder continued, his gaze studying her with a new shine. "Thirty-one years old and single."

He said that in a way that suggested he approved. But again, Emma felt something like a dull knife stabbing at her heart. "Guess I don't have much of a love life."

His eyes held hers a little too long on that last note. "Tried any dating sites?"

"Wow, Detective, you sound as if *you're* casing me for a date or something. Do you hang out on match-up sites a lot?"

"If I did," he said with a slow drawl that feathered its way down her spine, "I'm guessing I wouldn't find any information on one Emma Langston there."

"You'd be right on that, but what would it matter? Seems you know more about me than I know myself. Like I said, I don't date very much."

"And you remembered that, at least."

"I'm remembering odd things," she admitted. "Any deep, dark secrets in my background check?"

"I did find one thing interesting," he said, his voice calm and controlled and clear. But he hesitated.

"What?" she asked, her heart pumping. "I can handle it. Just tell me."

"Emma, you were a foster child. You went through the system from the time you were five and lived in several different homes around the Houston area."

Emma grabbed the blanket covering her, her fingers digging into the lightweight fabric. Her heart went cold, vague memories echoing through the pain in her head. "I… I don't…remember. Why can't I remember?"

"Hopefully it will come to you," he said, his tone soft and low. "You also have a gap in your background. Almost a whole year between high school and college. But you would have just aged out so maybe you took off and stayed low until you decided to work your way through college."

Emma stared him down, her mind like a massive cobweb. She didn't remember very much, but that missing year seemed to jump right out at her, like a bad clown trying to scare her. Shivers made goose bumps on her arms.

"Any record of what happened to my parents? How did I wind up in the system?"

"I haven't found anything on that yet," he admitted. "But I found something in your wallet. A picture of a couple and an address on the back. But no names. Maybe they were your birth parents."

He pulled out a photo encased in clear plastic and handed it to her. "Do you recognize them?"

Emma stared at the couple, the term *birth parents* chilling her like ice water. The woman had a classic bob haircut, grayish and simple. The man wore glasses and had a nice smile. Something tugged at Emma when she recognized her own handwriting in the hastily jotted address. A push and pull that she didn't want to explore. She took in breaths, a sense of foreboding making it hard to find air.

"Did you contact these people based on that address?" she asked Ryder.

"Not yet." He watched her staring at the photo. "But I have someone down south who does the same kind of work you do. He's waiting for us to give him the go-ahead to question them."

"Don't," she said. "Not yet. I can't remember these people so…let's see if I can figure it all out before we approach them."

"Are you afraid?"

Her pulse bumped into an erratic beat. "I don't understand what I am right now. Maybe they were my clients? But why would I carry their picture in my wallet?"

"They could tell us why."

"Not yet," she said, her gut holding her back. "I'm a PI. I keep quiet on a lot of things. What if I came here investigating those people?"

"Do you think that?"

"I can't be sure. But before we involve them, I'd like to hear what your friend finds out."

Ryder took the picture back and then gave her a blank stare. "What are you leaving out? What's going on with you? You've wanted to get out there and get at it, and now you're holding back on me."

"I told you, I don't remember much," she replied. "I feel it in my gut, though. I had to have come here looking for someone. I must be looking for a certain person. That couple could be my clients or they could be part of the problem."

He sat up and nodded, but he didn't push her on anything else. "I talked to a source who saw you in the Triple B. Said you were asking a lot of questions about underage teens. Does that ring a bell?"

Her heart skipped a beat. "Can you find my cell phone, please?"

"Emma?"

"I told you, I want to leave the hospital and I'll do it, with or without you."

"Don't be foolish. How can you solve this thing when you can't even remember much past your name and occupation?"

She bit her lip and hit her fists against the blanket in frustration. "Would you leave, please?"

"I'm trying to help you," he said, his own aggravation darkening his golden eyes to burnished brown. "Let me work this thing out."

"It might be too late," she cried out. "And don't ask me how I know that."

Ryder got up and touched her hand. "Look, my partner and I are working on this. There are some bad elements at the Triple B and we're trying to break up a dangerous ring of criminals. You don't need to be in the middle of that."

"I'd say I'm already in the middle of that," she retorted.

"I'll keep beating at the bushes and I'll report back to you every day. How about that?"

Knowing he'd come here to see her made Emma feel better and also made her let go of some of her hesitations. But she had no intention of lying here like a sitting duck.

"They'll find me," she said. "I saw a brief report on the evening news late last night. About me."

Anger shot over his features. "What?"

"They didn't name me but they reported an unidentified woman being attacked behind the Triple B and that she was in a local hospital." She swallowed, wishing she hadn't told him that, but he'd find out soon enough. "The report indicated the Triple B is a very dangerous place. Especially for vulnerable young women. Then they talked to a local businessman named Bobby something who ranted about crime in that area."

Ryder shook his head and groaned. "Bobby Doug Manchester. A lawyer and a real estate tycoon who's always griping about the crime around that part of town. Speculators think he's gearing up to run for office one day. Reporters listen to the police scanners. On slow nights, they go for any scrap of news even when they don't have all the facts, and Bobby Doug listens in and rants on about crime in his district since he'd like to buy out the vacant buildings around there. He probably tipped off the reporters."

Ryder figured that was what his early morning visit to

the station earlier had been all about. The self-righteous Bobby Doug hounded the locals on a regular basis.

"Well, I'm that scrap of news and the man made it clear he wants the lowlifes off the streets of Dallas," she replied, her tone calming now. "I'm a PI investigating some sort of case that somebody wants to keep me from investigating, and someone else is paying me to do that. I don't need some ambitious businessman mentioning me by name so he can gain points. Another reason why I need to get out of here."

Ryder stood over her, worry clouding his face. "Part of the report you heard in the news is correct, Emma. I'm doing my best to get rid of that bad element at the bar, so I don't need the press or Bobby Doug snooping around. But then again, maybe someone wants the press involved enough to scare you away. Do you believe those two were going to kill you?"

"I'm pretty sure of it," she said, nodding. "I must have asked too many questions about something they didn't want me to know."

Ryder lowered his head and gave her a direct stare. "Or you were close to finding *someone* they didn't want you to find."

"I need my cell phone," she said, turning to get out of bed.

"We didn't find a phone on you or near you. And if we had, it would have gone to the lab."

"But it might help me remember something or find out why I came here. Are you sure?"

"We didn't find anything like that near where you were attacked. No purse or phone, nothing except your wallet… and a weapon."

"I carry a gun?"

"Yes, and you've got a permit for that. Already cleared.

Your gun is safe back at headquarters in the evidence room. It hasn't been fired recently. Clean as a whistle."

Another strong memory of trying to get to the gun. "I rarely have to use the thing."

He looked in the locker next to the bathroom. "Your wallet is right here in the bag with your clothes, but we cataloged and photographed what we found. The crime scene techs didn't find much in the alley, but they did dust the Dumpster where you fell."

She took in a gulp of air. "I was shoved against the Dumpster."

"You remembered?"

"Yes, someone shoved me. They held me but I fought back until one of them found the sweet spot on that bat." She held tight to the blanket and sheet. "Somebody shouted just as the bat came down. I managed to move my head, but obviously it still made contact."

"Another odd memory."

"Do you believe me, Detective Palladin?"

"Should I believe you, PI Emma Langston?"

"Why would I lie? I'm remembering bits and pieces. That's all I've got for now. Why don't you go Dumpster diving and see if Bounce and Ounce threw away my phone?"

Ryder settled in the nearby chair but never really answered any of her questions. She didn't blame him for doubting her, but it stung either way. Frustration made her lash out. "What do you think?"

"Bounce and Ounce would have cleaned up the scene if Pierce hadn't sent them scurrying. Those two have heavy records on petty crime and a nice history of several assaults, so they'd have no qualms about murdering anyone. But we can't find them to get their side of things. There wouldn't have been any trace of you ever being there if they'd succeeded."

"You think they have my phone?"

He held up a finger. "I'm going to send Pierce back out there with the techs to check the Dumpster again. They would have checked it the other night—or should have. They might find something new with today's trash dump, though."

"I must have had a car. How else could I get there?"

"Do you remember a car?"

She closed her eyes, then hit her fists against the sheets. "No. Nothing. Maybe I took the DART."

She watched as he texted someone. How could she remember the transit system and not the people in that photo? Who were they? Did they hire her?

Ryder didn't notice her inner agitation. "My partner will know if they found your car, but we didn't find it last night. Bounce could have hidden it and your phone."

"I remember a dark parking lot. A long street."

"That's something at least." He finished the text, his eyes on her again. "If we find an abandoned vehicle nearby we can trace the license and registration and see if it belongs to you."

"Yep. First thing I'd try."

"Funny, that memory of yours. Selective."

"The doctor said it could be this way."

"I read up on amnesia, so I reckon he's got you all figured out."

He was calculating, and her not having a phone with her wasn't adding up. Not in her disoriented thoughts either. "Maybe I purposely left my phone in the car. You know, to keep them from seeing something I'd saved there."

"We'll go with that for now. That, or they have the phone and already know what's on it."

"Okay." Her heart was sinking by the minute while her pulse seemed to be rising. "I need to get out of here, Ryder."

Ryder went back to the locker again. "When you're able." Then he went into the bathroom, probably checking the place out for weapons or things she'd hidden, since he obviously didn't believe her or think she should leave the hospital.

She was about to show him that she was able to get up and go but the door opened and a janitor entered with a big cart. "I need to clean the AC filters."

Emma glanced toward where Ryder had gone still beyond the bathroom door, his hand on his weapon, a finger to his mouth. Then she glanced back at the man and shook her head.

"Excuse me?" she said, stalling. "I don't see any filter vents in here."

The man didn't elaborate.

Ryder didn't wait. He whirled around the door, his gun drawn and aimed at the man. "Show me some ID."

The surprised intruder took one look at Ryder and pushed the cart toward him, then managed to tug at the door and run down the long hospital hallway.

"Don't move, Emma," Ryder called out. Then he hurried down the hall ordering the nurses to call security. "Lock this place down," he shouted. "Now."

THREE

Ryder moved down the stairwell at a breakneck speed, his boots hitting steel as he chased after the man who'd just tried to attack Emma. When a shot rang out and missed Ryder by inches, he grunted and picked up speed. They made it to the bottom floor of the sprawling hospital. Ryder listened as a door opened and shut with a thud and a bang.

By the time he got outside to the loading dock, the man was gone in a sea of linen trucks and official vehicles.

Calling in a description, Ryder hurried back up to check on Emma. After a thorough search by both hospital security and several police officers, the lockdown was lifted.

Pierce showed up and took a report. "No sign of the man you described, Palladin. He's long gone. But we got people looking."

"Keep at it," Ryder replied while they stood in the hallway in front of Emma's room. "I'll stand guard. And let me know what our people find at the Dumpster behind the bar. Tell them to go over every inch of that alley and the side streets."

"So…you're staying here tonight?" Pierce asked, his hazel eyes moving over Ryder's face as if he had the plague or something.

"Yeah," Ryder said. "You have a problem with that?"

"No, but we have people for that."

"I'm people. I can guard her door if I want to."

"That's the part that's got me confused. You wanting to."

"What does that mean?"

Pierce pushed a gangly hand through his straight brown bangs. "You never want to…get this close to someone, Ryder. You make it a point not to want to, know what I mean?"

"Look, I'm protecting a woman who got hit over the head by two very nasty men. That's not exactly a fair fight."

Realization lightened Pierce's eyes like a bulb in a dark hallway coming to life. "Oh, now I get it. You're all about things being fair in life."

"Yeah, you got a problem with that, too?"

"Nope. But we both know that ain't how life works."

Ryder got in Pierce's face, the frustrations of the day raging through his system. "I'm staying here tonight, Mr. Philosophy. Get over it."

Pierce shrugged and whirled to leave. "Don't worry. While you're being a Guardian of the Galaxy, I'll be doing all the grunge work on finding the car, the phone, the bad guys. You know, little details that make up a case."

"Thanks. So sweet of you."

Ryder turned back to Emma's room to find her glaring at him. "I don't need you to stay here with me. I need you to get me out of here. I've been through tests, I'm remembering more by the minute and my head has finally stopped throbbing like a sore thumb. I'm okay to leave."

She'd obviously heard his conversation with Pierce. "The doctor thinks you need to stay awhile longer."

She fell back against the pillow. "Okay."

Ryder knew she was biding her time. If he closed just

one eye, she'd bolt right past him. Shaking his head, he said, "I'll just bunk right here in this comfortable recliner."

"No. You stay outside. Watch the door."

"No. I'll stay right here. In this recliner. Throw me a blanket, will you?"

"How did you get so stubborn?"

"That's a long story."

"I have nothing but time and a blank mind."

Ryder shook his head. "You realize that what happened here earlier was another attempt to get to you, right?"

"How can I not realize that? I told you they'd find me. If you hadn't been here—"

Her aggravated blue-green gaze rippled across his soul like undercurrents of warm, inviting water. Ryder couldn't go down in that current.

Then she spoke again. "You set me up nicely for that admission, didn't you?"

"I didn't set up anything. That's the facts, and you know it. But now I agree that we need to get you out of here. I will do that, but I need to figure some things out first. So until then, we stay here. Together."

She tossed him the blanket. "Do you snore?"

"Never."

"Can we order in?"

"What do you want?"

"I told you—a cheeseburger."

He could seriously fall for this woman.

"No, we can't order that in because I'm pretty sure you'd regret it. Probably wise to eat soft foods not so heavy on your system for a few days."

She slanted her eyes. "Are you speaking from experience?"

"Could be."

He could read her enough to know that she didn't want

to back down either, but she looked tired and defeated. "Okay, I'll eat more Jell-O and scrambled eggs. But once I'm out of here—"

"I know just the place," he replied, grinning. "And I'll even buy."

"It's a date," Emma said. Then she shook her head. "I mean, not a date. It's not a date."

Ryder gave her a mock-sad face. "Okay, I get it. It's a nondate date. A make-good-on-a-promise kind of date. Because you and me—not a thing. Not gonna happen. Am I right?"

"So right," she said, her expression determined. "So right." Then she shifted into not-gonna-happen overdrive. "Even if it did, I'd probably forget that it did."

"You are cruel," he said, wagging his finger at her. "But if and when that not-gonna-happen happens, I'll make sure you remember."

After she closed her gaping mouth, she recovered nicely. "Stop talking."

Ryder did a zip swipe across his lips. But he wished they could go on a real date. Wished it and then dismissed it.

Two hours later, Emma woke up to find Ryder still in the recliner, watching over her.

Even though he wouldn't let her have a cheeseburger, he looked just as yummy as ever, sitting there with his long, jean-clad legs stretched out in front of him and his shirt sleeves rolled up to show off his tanned, hair-dusted forearms.

"Hello, sunshine," he said, his voice husky. "How are you feeling?"

"Like I'm under house arrest."

"That bad, huh? What can I do to help?"

That was a loaded question, considering his sleepy,

husky voice and that silky, curly hair. But she thought long and hard on how to answer it.

"Tell me that long story about you," she said, wanting to fill her mind with details. Wanting to remember what she needed to find. "I want to hear about your life. Maybe not thinking about mine will help me relax."

"It's not that exciting," he said, after taking a sip of soda from a can the nurse must have brought him. "Grew up on a ranch that's been around since Custer's last stand and pretty much farmed and worked the land until I became a cop. Crops, livestock, including cattle and horses, the usual Texas overkill."

"And you loved it, right?"

"I did. I do. I still live there. I sleep in town a lot at headquarters but I get back to the Palace as often as I can."

"The Palace?" She snorted a laugh. "Think highly of ourselves, do we?"

"Someone named it that long ago and it stuck. It's always been the Palladin Ranch. Big and bold, but we ain't fancy. Just my mother and my younger sister and me. We lost my dad a few years ago, but they still live in the main house. I have a cabin around the bend from them."

"I'm sorry about your dad," she said, meaning it.

"Yeah, me, too." He shrugged. "I went into law enforcement because of him. Because of what happened to him."

Noting the darkness following that statement, she asked, "What did happen...with your dad?"

Thinking a heart attack or stroke, she was shocked when he took a breath and told her the truth. "He was a sheriff. All my life, he was larger than life. Off duty one night and stopped to get gas. Robbed and his truck taken. He tried to stop them but they shot him. He died at the scene."

Emma put a hand to her mouth. "Ryder, I'm so sorry. I shouldn't have pried."

"It's okay," he said, his smile full of regret. "They caught the man who did it. A career criminal. Won't see life on the streets for a long time."

"Good."

"I always wanted to follow in his footsteps, so I joined the police academy. I wanted to stop the hard-core criminals."

"You mean the ones like your father's killer?"

"Yep."

"So you asked to work Vice?"

"Yep."

He'd told her more than he'd wanted to tell.

Emma wanted to know more, but his gaze shouted to let it go. "Where is this palatial ranch?"

"Northwest of Fort Worth between Lake Worth and Denton."

She stopped teasing. "I know Denton. I remember Denton."

"You'll figure all of this out soon."

"I hope." She noticed he didn't like to talk in specifics. Because somewhere between Lake Worth and Denton could mean many out-of-the-way places.

Having him near had helped her take her mind off things, but having him near also meant she was still in the thick of this mess. "What do we do now?"

"We wait out the night and see if you remember anything else. Maybe the doc will spring you tomorrow."

She sat up, a slight throb moving through her temple. "Ryder, when someone is missing, we both know the first few hours are critical. And I've already wasted close to forty-eight hours in here."

"Did you remember something?"

"No, I didn't remember precisely but…I have this urgency in my gut and it's telling me I need to get back out there. I have good instincts. I know that somehow."

"You can't do anything right now regarding what we might find out there." He checked his watch, then pulled out his cell. "I had one of the techs do a search for any underage teens reported missing in the last week. I'll put a fire under him and see if he's found any names."

Emma sat watching him work. He had a way about him—smooth, in control, calm—that got other people moving. She'd heard him passing insults with his partner, but the mirth in both their eyes told her they trusted and depended on each other.

Would they help her? Really help her? Or were they using this as part of their sting operation? More evidence against the lowlifes who hung around the Triple B?

She'd also heard his partner questioning Ryder about watching out for her. As in, he didn't get too close to his subjects or his suspects?

Was he getting close to her, or staying close to her in hopes of finding out what she knew?

Hard to say. Emma closed her eyes and tried to picture her life coming back together, not in puzzle pieces that moved through her head and made it ache all over again. She needed the pieces to fit and make sense.

But nothing more came to the surface.

I'm Emma Langston. I'm a private investigator from Galveston. I have no idea why I'm here. Why? Why did I go to that bar? Who am I looking for?

And why did Bounce and Ounce try to kill her?

Ryder closed his phone. "We have several names and photos of missing teens. This is just in the last week or so. Want to look at them?"

She swallowed, nodded, feared the worst. "Yes."

But after looking at the photos that came through on his

phone and reading the names of the five missing teens—three girls and two boys—in the Dallas/Fort Worth area, Emma fell back against her pillow and closed her eyes for a few seconds before opening them to stare over at Ryder.

"I don't recognize any of them. And the names don't ring a bell. What if one of them is the one I'm trying to find, Ryder?"

"People are already on these cases," he said. "But that doesn't mean someone didn't hire you."

She went cold inside. "What if the parents haven't listed the teen as missing yet? What if they thought I'd find their child right away?"

"No parent would do that," he reminded her. "They call the locals right away."

"And if that didn't work?"

"They'd call you," he admitted. "Maybe they called you and the locals don't know that."

"That would mean the parents have to be frantic by now."

He put down his phone. "You look tired, and you won't be able to focus if you don't heal. So rest, Emma. Just lie back and go to sleep."

"I can't sleep."

"Try."

"Has anyone questioned Bounce and Ounce?"

"We've tried. Unavailable. The Triple B has gone on the quiet. No one will dare talk out of fear of getting a bat to their head. But we're watching the place even more now."

A nurse came in and gave her a pill. "Just a mild pain pill." After examining Emma, she asked, "How's your head pain on a scale of one to ten?"

Emma held the pill cup and replied, "Maybe a three."

"That's a good sign but take the acetaminophen anyway."

Emma didn't want to take anything that would muddle her memory even more, but the nurse urged her to so she could sleep.

"You people never let up."

"Our job," the smiling nurse said. "But you're improving so much I think you'll be able to leave soon."

After the nurse left, Emma looked at Ryder. "Leave? And where do I go from here? I've been so intent on getting out I haven't considered if I had a hotel room anywhere."

When he didn't respond, she said, "But then, you've already checked the area hotels, right?"

"Right. So far, your name hasn't come up, but we'll keep looking. Maybe you checked in under an alias?"

She actually snorted a laugh. "And you expect me to remember that alias?"

"No. We'll keep at it."

"I have to find a place to stay," she said, the thought jarring her head all over again. "I can't go home not knowing."

Ryder slanted his gaze toward her, his head tilted. "Well, wherever that is, I won't be far away. I want to solve this, too. And I want to bring in Bounce and Ounce and slam the jail door on them once and for all."

"I've given you extra work," she said, glad to know he was on her side.

"Keeps me out of trouble."

Emma drifted off to sleep with the memory of his determined look and definite tone in her mind.

Ryder was that kind of guy.

He did things the old-fashioned way.

The cowboy way.

Ryder woke with a grunt.

He'd heard something. A slamming noise followed by a crash.

And where was Emma?

Bolting out of the recliner, he called out, "Emma?"

"In here."

The bathroom door was closed.

"Are you okay?"

"Yes," came the muffled reply. "But that man on the floor isn't."

Ryder whirled when he heard a moan. Rushing to the other side of the bed, he found a tall, athletic man with short platinum hair holding a hand to his head. Ryder drew his gun and yanked the man up.

"Don't move or I will shoot you," he said, showing the man his badge before he shoved him against the wall. "Put your hands up."

The man moaned and did as he asked. "She tried to kill me."

Emma walked out of the bathroom, her hair disheveled, her eyes flashing. "Well, you tried to stick a needle in my arm. I don't like needles."

Ryder frisked the man and found a knife and a hidden pistol strapped to his ankle. Spotting the syringe on the floor by the bed, he read the man his rights and cuffed him.

Whirling the man around, Ryder looked at Emma. "Are you really okay?"

"Yes," she said, sinking down onto the bed. "I woke up and this *visitor* came at me with a needle full of clear liquid. I kicked out and hit him toward his…uh…midsection then threw the water jug in his face."

"And she jammed me with that bed tray thing," the man said on a whine and a glare.

"She's good about taking care of things," Ryder said with a grin at the overturned tray. But his heart flipped and flopped in a delayed panic. He shouldn't have dozed and he should have stayed outside in front of the door. But he'd wanted to be near *her*. Just one more reason to stay away from *her*. Giving Emma a warning stare, he slammed the man back against the wall. "Talk."

"I got nothin' to say."

"You'll talk, sooner or later," Ryder said on a soft promise. "I'm thinking soon you'll be singing like a little bird."

No ID and an unyielding, cold, dead stare.

"I want a lawyer."

"Oh, I'm sure you'll get one. But for now, you're mine."

In a matter of minutes, the hospital once again swarmed with officers. After Pierce and his men took the assailant away, Ryder finally turned to where the doctor was checking Emma.

"Doc, she seems okay to me. I mean, she took down a man who could have easily snapped her neck."

Dr. Sherrington didn't smile. "Our patient had improved dramatically but she still has memory issues."

"I'm taking her to my ranch," Ryder said, daring either one of them to argue. "My mother happens to be a retired ER nurse."

"How convenient," the doctor quipped. He looked down at Emma. "Do you want this man to take you away from me?"

"More than you'll ever know," Emma replied. "But he could have cleared it with me first."

FOUR

Since Emma insisted she was leaving with or without the doctor's release, the hospital signed her out and Ryder followed her wheelchair. The orderly pushing Emma's chair had been handpicked by the doctor, and Ryder had two patrol officers flanking them.

They made it to Ryder's big Chevy without incident, but he kept his gun at the ready until the orderly had helped her into the dark navy truck.

After thanking the nervous hospital attendant, Ryder turned to the two officers. "Thanks. Let me know if you find anything regarding the man we arrested tonight. I'll be in to question him later."

"Do you want an escort, Detective?"

"No," Ryder said. "I'll be taking the back roads."

He got inside and glanced over at Emma. She now wore an old gray sweat suit he'd had stashed in the truck. At least the garments were clean, even if she'd had to tie the pants tight and the hoodie hung loose on her. He'd have to find her some more clothes. Meantime, he'd called ahead to warn his mother and sister that they were about to have a houseguest.

"How are you?" he asked once she was settled in.

"I'm having the best time of my life," she said, her tone

solid deadpan, her hands hidden under the cuffs of the hoodie. "Life in Dallas is so much fun I can hardly contain myself."

Ryder cranked the big truck and the motor roared to life. Her sarcasm matched his own to perfection, which made his frown dig deeper into his bones. "Well, you're about to leave the city for a while. You can rest and heal in a secluded, safe place."

"I appreciate being sprung," she said, "but I don't intend to rest. Do you have Wi-Fi and modern communications?"

"No, we get by with soup cans wired together and yodeling across the woods."

"Funny." She stared out the truck window. "They'll keep coming. Someone wants me out of the way."

"Well, I'll keep pushing right back," he replied. "We can sit down together tomorrow and try to figure this out, Emma. But you can't go out there without having a plan and a sense of what you're getting yourself into."

"I can't remember *what* I'm into, Ryder. It's frustrating."

Ryder wanted to reach out to her but knew better. He had to convince her not to run. She'd do it. He could see it in her eyes. "I'll help you. Whatever you stumbled into surely has something to do with my case. It might even give us the break we need."

"Whatever I can do to help. Lose my memory. Regain my memory. Badger you. Pray. Rant. Get back at it."

"Hey," he said, touching her arm. "Hey, do not do that. They'll kill you. They've already tried three times now. And you dead won't save whoever you're trying to help."

Emma gave him a hard stare and winced as she shook her head. "I'm well aware of that, so why would I want to put your family in danger, too?"

"My family will be okay, trust me."

Had she picked up on the panic in his voice and misread it? Well, he couldn't protect her if she went rogue on him. And he couldn't solve his case if she got in his way.

But Ryder knew his concerns stretched a little further than just duty. He kind of had a thing for her. She was tough and pretty in a striking way and she knew her stuff—or at least she knew the ins and outs of life on the streets and dealing with criminals. She'd fought against two of the meanest lowlifes in Dallas. He liked the entire package, but he wanted to get to know the woman inside that tough package. That unexplainable need shook him up more than anything else that had happened over the last few days.

Yeah, he had a thing for a woman who couldn't remember why she was here or why someone would want her gone. And he was taking that woman home to his ranch.

There were all kinds of wrongs in that scenario.

But only one right. He didn't have a choice. He wouldn't toss her out there to the wolves.

"You aren't sure about this, are you?" she asked when he didn't say anything else, her hair falling all around her face in an auburn cascade.

"I'm sure of one thing. I wasn't about to leave you in that hospital. Now quit trying to outsmart me. You won't win."

"Sure of *yourself*, too, aren't you?"

"I told you, what I'm doing is the right thing for now. You can't do this alone. I'm in it all the way."

"I'm not too happy about that."

"Well, you can turn that pretty frown upside down. You'll be safe at the ranch. I have workers who carry weapons for all kinds of protection and…I have a mama who can pack some heat, too. Pretty sure my sister's had enough target practice to take down a longhorn if need be."

She absorbed that. "And then there's you."

"And then there's me, yes. I'll be right there with you. Until we're done."

Emma pushed at her hair. The bandage on her head had been changed to a smaller one, and she'd passed most of the tests the doctor wanted her to pass. She was full of stubbornness, which meant she wouldn't back down until she found the truth.

They had that in common. Ryder figured they had a lot more in common, too. But he didn't have time to explore such things. He wanted the truth before he made any stupid moves.

He had a feeling once the dam on her memories opened up she'd take off like a jackrabbit. And he might not ever see her again. Dead or alive.

He wanted her alive. So they could have that not-gonna-happen date that he wanted to happen.

Emma didn't say anything else. She leaned against the glass of the passenger-side window and watched the road.

She was mapping the road signs. He'd do the same if someone was taking him to a strange place.

He only hoped she didn't map her way off the ranch without him. That could become her last trip, and then they'd never have the answers they needed.

Emma squinted into the dark, tired from the drive and wondering why she didn't have any energy. But it had already been three days since she'd been hit over the head and left for dead in that alley. Trying to focus on the glowing interstate signs only made her dizzy. She'd figured enough to know they were heading west on I-30 but then he took the truck north above Fort Worth proper. From his vague description of the location, she knew the ranch had to be miles from either the Dallas area or Denton. She'd have to remember the county roads, too.

Grateful to be alive and away from the hospital, where anyone could sneak in and kill her, Emma sighed and tried not to think about the man at the wheel of this monster truck. So she focused on the road signs and wondered about the place where this mysterious man lived. What would that be like?

Soon, she saw signs for Lake Worth and the Trinity River, but Ryder guided the truck away from the subdivisions around the lake and kept going northwest until he finally turned onto a deserted road.

"You do like to get away from the city," she said. "We'll be in West Texas if you don't pull over soon."

"Impatient to see where I live?"

She lifted up too fast. Dizziness made her blink. "No, just ready to be out of this truck."

While Ryder turned the truck to the right and slowly guided it up a long gravel lane, she thanked God that his partner had found her. She'd have to thank Pierce Daughtry next time she saw him. If she ever saw him again. When she'd asked Ryder for help, Emma had not factored in his bringing her home to Mama. She'd agreed to come here only to get out of the hospital. She knew how to find her way off a ranch, even one that was gated and apparently had an alarm system and security lights shining on every corner of the house and yard.

The house was two-storied and huge, but it wasn't a stuffy old palace at all. It looked like a farmhouse but stretched on both sides like a large plantation house. The stark white wooden walls contrasted nicely with the darkly varnished shutters lining the windows. A massive porch wrapped around the bottom level, and smaller balconies finished out the top floor. Two huge mushrooming live oaks bookcased each side of the house and shaded the porches. Crape myrtles lined the driveway and the fence lines. Roses blinked underneath the security lights and heavy shrubs added protection along the white wooden fence lines. It might be tricky to find her way out of here.

"Nice digs, Detective."

"This is where my mom and sister live. I have a cabin down near the pond."

He had mentioned that, but she turned to him as he pulled the roaring truck up to the side of the house. "Oh, a lone wolf?"

"A man can only take so much bickering and chattering about hairstyles, shoes, gaining weight and losing boyfriends."

"Do you actually allow you sister to date?"

"I wouldn't call it *allow*. More like I don't have much choice, but I have them all vetted and if I don't like what I see, I have my way of stating my case."

"Does your sister know you do background checks on her boyfriends?"

"The subject hasn't come up."

Probably because he'd threaten any man after his sister within an inch of his life if Ryder didn't like the man.

Emma didn't understand her keen need to banter with this cowboy. But something was sure stewing between them. Probably just the apprehension connected to this case, all those variables that should add up but didn't. Was it natural to want to kiss him and then leave him?

I can't think about him. Not in that way. He's here to help me until I don't need him anymore.

Then she had to wonder. *Is that what I do to people? Use them and lose them so things don't get messy?*

"Hey, are you okay?" Ryder asked, jarring her out of the non-memories that held back with a sad edge.

"Just taking it all in. I don't like depending on other people."

"I can see that, but could you just let me help you? Don't try to do this on your own when you're still confused and disoriented, okay?"

Could he read her mind? Of course. He was a detective after all. Used to people figuring out ways to get away from him.

"Am I under house arrest here, too?"

"No, but you are under protective custody. My protection."

"Not your custody, though. You can't force me to stay here."

Before he could respond, the front door of the house swung open and an older woman with shoulder-length grayish hair came out onto the porch. "Ryder, bring her on inside. It's hot and muggy out here."

Emma glanced at the truck's still-glowing dashboard clock. It had taken almost an hour to get here. "Midnight. Your mother is up late."

"She never sleeps," he said. Then he got out of the truck and came around to her door.

"Must run in the family," Emma retorted, opening the door before he could.

"Hello there, I'm Nancy Palladin," the woman said as she greeted Emma by placing both of her warm hands over the one Emma extended. Nancy wore a blue T-shirt over worn jeans and boots.

"Hi," Emma said, fatigue tugging at her. "Thank you so much for allowing me to…stay here."

"Nonsense," Nancy said. "We don't get many visitors, and it's a rare day when my son brings home a pretty woman."

"Mama," Ryder said, clearly uncomfortable with that comment, "this is Emma. Is her room ready?"

"Of course," his mother replied, letting go of Emma's hand to take her by the arm. "C'mon in and we'll get you settled. We can get acquainted in the morning."

Emma followed Mrs. Palladin into the house where the huge entryway led to big rooms on both sides, one a den with a massive fireplace and the other a formal living room. The wide staircase stretched beyond the entry and central hallway.

The house was lit with muted lamps here and there but Emma had seen enough to tell it was well maintained and comfortable, and it smelled of spices and lavender.

"We have two guest rooms downstairs," Nancy explained. "I'll show you where you'll be staying." She stopped and waited for Emma. "I elevated the pillows on your bed. That's important after a head trauma. No reading, online browsing or texting, and no exercising. If you wake with a headache, take your meds. You might have trouble sleeping, but that's normal. And your emotions will be all over the map, so just go with it for a few days. Mainly you need to rest."

"I feel as if I'm back in the hospital," Emma said with a smile. "Ryder told me you're a retired nurse."

"And a bossy one," Ryder added, nodding. "Mom, she doesn't have a phone or a laptop, so she has no choice but to rest."

"Good." Nancy turned to Ryder. "And I fixed up the room across from Emma, just as you asked."

"What?" Emma said, turning to face Ryder. "You're staying here tonight?"

"Yes," he said, daring her to complain.

She complained anyway. "I don't need you across the hall from me."

"Yes, you do," he retorted. "It's late and you need to rest. My sister, Stephanie, found you some pajamas and an outfit for tomorrow. I'll take you to your room."

"I can take care of things myself," she retorted, trying to find a suitable reason to ditch him.

"I'm going to be across the hall," he replied, stubborn all over his face. "And that's that." Then to push the matter home, he added, "My family is here, too. I have to watch out for all of you."

Since he had a point, Emma didn't want to make a scene in front of the man's mother. "All right," she said. "I just want to go to sleep."

Then she turned to Nancy. "Thank you again. I'll be more human tomorrow, I hope."

Nancy chuckled and glanced at her son. "I understand so much more now than I did before."

Emma saw the exchange between mother and son. But she wasn't sure she liked what that exchange implied.

FIVE

Emma woke up to sunshine.

Then she sat up and glanced around, disorientation once again pouring over her in a wave of panic.

She had to remember where she was.

Oh, right. At the Palace. His home. Or rather, his mother's home. So they owned a ranch and yet his father had been a sheriff and his mother had been a nurse. He had one sister who was probably practicing to be a superhero.

A hardworking normal Texas family that obviously had deep roots on this land, but they'd chosen high-stress jobs away from the ranch.

Did they all have a need to serve? Were people really that good? Or did that death wish thing run in the family? Not that a nurse would want a death wish, but his mother had probably seen the worst of life and death.

Stop rambling about Ryder and get up.

Because the sooner she gained her strength, the quicker she could be out there, searching.

But for what? For whom?

Maybe Ryder was right. She couldn't go off half-cocked with no information and no direction. And yet, her gut told her this was an urgent matter. But she had one of the best at her disposal. The man worked Vice. What more did she need to know to trust him?

A lot more. Did she have trust issues? Why couldn't she remember?

Emma pulled back the heavy down spread, her gaze taking in the floral colors of the understated room. Blues, yellows, tans, creams. Some greenery—live plants at the windows. She liked that and the soothing, calm tone of this room. Two huge windows covered with creamy drapes enticed her across the soft, plush peach-colored carpet. The bright sun made her head bump and ache, but Emma needed to see that sun. She'd had a restless night, in and out of sleep and dreams.

She pulled the drapes back and looked out onto a sprawling backyard that held a pool and what appeared to be an outdoor kitchen complete with a huge stove and grill. Beyond the pool, potted plants sat in colorful stone pots and several groupings of outdoor furniture surrounded the patio area. The white fence she'd seen last night continued on each side of the wide, rectangular yard, and a big gate opened onto the fields and meadow beyond. She could just see the horses and cattle grazing on the other side of the fence. A stable and barn stood off to one side of the big pasture. A garage completed the other side of the compound.

Taking in a deep breath, Emma wished she'd come here under different circumstances, but it couldn't be helped. And she didn't have time to lollygag in her bedroom.

Her stomach growled and she realized she hadn't had a decent meal in days. Time to remedy that. She took a quick shower and looked in the closet by the bathroom. She found a few casual clothes and picked out a turquoise T-shirt that had a rodeo logo on it and a pair of capri-style jeans that would have to work with her boots. The jeans were a little snug but wearable.

These clothes must belong to Ryder's sister. Stephanie. Yes, that was her name. Seventeen and going on twenty-seven, the way Ryder had described her.

Emma finished getting dressed, glad that she hadn't had a dizzy spell, and combed her hair with the brush she'd found on the bathroom counter, her gaze hitting on the bandage on the right side of her head above her temple. Paleness and fatigue made her look like death warmed over, but she reminded herself she wasn't dead. She could feel the pain of being hit, so why couldn't she remember what had happened to bring her here?

When a knock sounded on the door, she dropped the brush and chided herself for being so skittish. "Coming."

Emma expected to see Ryder standing there with that intense look that worked its way through her system each time she gazed into his eyes. Instead, she saw a younger version of his mother.

"Stephanie?" she asked, smiling.

The girl bounced into the room. "You know my name?"

"Ryder told me about you."

Emma took in Stephanie's riding pants and button-up shirt, tall boots and dark ponytail. She had some of Ryder in her, too.

"I'm guessing he told you I'm a brat and spoiled and that he does checks on anyone I bring home, right?"

Emma had to laugh. "Well, that's close."

Stephanie slung her ponytail and grinned. "He's a good brother but just a tad controlling."

"Hmm, I think that's what older brothers are obligated to be, right?"

"I don't know. Do you have siblings?"

Emma balked and Stephanie hit her hand against her head. "I'm so sorry. My bad. Ignore me. Mama wanted to let you know breakfast is ready since we heard you moving around in here."

"That's okay and I'm starving," Emma said, letting the earlier comment go. She didn't think she had any siblings and her gut wasn't burning, so she'd worry about that later.

She might not have any brothers or sisters, but she did know that thinking about that and family brought back that shred of regret and sadness that kept reaching toward her brain.

Emma pushed that away, her mind uneasy with what she might be holding back, what she might be afraid to remember. "Where's Ryder?" she asked as Stephanie led her to the kitchen.

"He went into work. Something about a new lead."

Emma stopped short. Ryder had gone off without her. Without even letting her know. What kind of lead?

She didn't ask Stephanie since the girl wouldn't have a clue because Ryder probably didn't talk much about work with his sister.

But when he got back, Emma intended to grill him good.

"Morning," Nancy said from the kitchen up the hallway. "C'mon and let's eat. You must be so hungry for good food."

"Yes," Emma said, the smell of bacon and coffee overtaking her anger at Ryder.

"We have eggs, bacon, grits and biscuits. Ryder said to tell you he'll be back by lunch."

"And I bet he also told you both to watch over me so I don't try to leave, didn't he?"

Both Nancy and Stephanie looked at her and then looked at each other.

"Of course he did, darlin'," Nancy said, one hand on her hip. "Ryder knows women too well. But he might have to rethink that with you."

Emma wanted to bolt away from Nancy Palladin's motherly stare, but she needed food. Then she could decide how to plan her exit strategy. But she would behave for now. "Don't worry, I'm not going anywhere. I think a day's rest will do me good."

"Smart woman," Nancy replied. "Now get you a plate and let's sit and chat. Stephanie and I want to get to know you."

Emma grabbed a biscuit and filled her plate to take it to the long breakfast table by another set of wide windows. "You do realize that I have amnesia?"

"Yes," Nancy said. She brought the coffee urn over to the table and poured three cups while Stephanie filled her own plate from the stove. "But I've dealt with amnesia patients before. Sometimes when you relax and just let go of whatever is holding back your memories, they come back on their own. You need rest and nourishment and nurturing right now, Emma."

"And protection," Emma said, her appetite disappearing. "I guess I'll be here for a while, won't I?"

"You'll be fine here," Stephanie said, her eyes wide with curiosity. "We've never had a private investigator here before. It's kind of cool."

Emma toyed with her eggs. "It won't be cool if I put all of you in danger."

"Is that what you're worried about?" Nancy asked, her coffee mug cupped between her hands.

"Isn't that important enough to worry about?" Emma

asked, that panic hovering over her like the humidity outside.

"Honey, this ain't our first rodeo," Nancy retorted. "We've held off bad guys before. Disgruntled workers, rustlers, poachers, trespassers, you name it, we can handle it."

"But these people are dangerous," Emma said, her mind grasping for the reason she knew that, beyond the obvious.

Nancy patted her hand. "Ryder puts himself in danger every day. We don't like it, but we have to accept it. You should understand that he's like a dog with a bone once he gets going on a case. He won't back down, and it's his nature to protect a woman in danger."

"And that's what scares me the most," Emma said.

Ryder pulled his truck up to the area by the garage and got out, fatigue weighing him down. He knew his mother was capable of running this ranch and he'd hired the best employees to help her do so, but he missed not being able to get out there and get his hands dirty. He took a rare weekend here or there to ride out with his mother or the ranch foreman, but some days after a particularly grueling case, he wished he could let go of the need to fight for justice and just live.

Really live.

Today had been one of those days.

He hated to have to go in there and face the three curious women who had probably been waiting all day, but he was tired and hungry and his mother had insisted he come to dinner since they had a guest.

His mother. Trying to set him up with an amnesic woman who was obviously caught up in something very dangerous.

That was called desperation.

But it kind of made him smile in spite of life.

So he greeted his golden retriever, Spur, and opened the back door, Spur running in ahead of him.

His mother and sister were nowhere to be found in the kitchen or the den, but someone was waiting for him.

Emma got up from a side chair and whirled to stare at him.

"You left without me."

Gauging the mood, he nodded slowly while Spur sniffed at her knuckles. "Yes."

"What kind of lead did you find?"

"I don't think I have to discuss that with you." He'd planned on it, but he was in an ornery mood and he didn't like being ambushed in his own house.

"But you will," she said. "If you've found something that can help me, I need to know."

Ryder stomped back toward the kitchen and rattled the refrigerator open to find a bottle of water. Then he downed half of it while she stood there with her red hair on fire and her boot tapping the floor.

"Well?"

"Not that you need to know, but what I found today was the body of one of my CIs. A kid named Junior who needed a break. Well, he got one all right. Somebody broke his neck because he talked to me yesterday and ID'd you from the bar. And hinted that Bounce and Ounce would kill him if he said more. He won't be saying anything now. He's in the morgue, with no one in the world to come and mourn his death."

Emma gasped and slipped onto a bar stool.

And because he'd been so harsh, Ryder handed her the rest of the water. "Here, drink this."

She took the bottle, her gaze holding him, her eyes wide with regret and a mist of pain. "I'm so sorry. I… I shouldn't have pushed you. I shouldn't be here. This is my fault but I don't know why and…I might not ever know."

Then she set the water down and turned and hurried out the back door. Spur glanced up at Ryder and took off after her.

SIX

Ryder's mother chose that moment to reappear.

Nancy stood with her hand on the newel post and called up the hallway to Ryder. "What's going on? Why'd you leave the door open? You know you'll let in flies and mosquitoes."

"I'll explain later." Ryder shook his head and hurried after Emma, afraid she'd take one of the ranch trucks and crash through the fence.

Instead, he found her at the back fence, staring at the horses and cattle, his once-faithful dog standing beside her and wagging his tail like a lovesick puppy.

"Emma," he called when he was almost to her. "You shouldn't be out here."

Spur shot him a glance and then lifted his brown eyes to Emma. And stayed with her. At least she had a new friend. And a good watchdog.

"Emma," he called again.

She didn't turn around. Instead she just stared out onto the pastures and hills, the hot afternoon wind whipping at her hair. She looked fragile and forlorn standing there in his sister's clothes, her head down, her arms wrapped against her as if she were cold.

Ryder didn't know why this woman seemed to tear at

his heartstrings, but he couldn't deny it. Maybe because she was alone and had lost some of her memories. Maybe because she'd been so tough and she had a purpose that seemed to be driving her. Or maybe because she knew something that he thought he needed to know for this investigation. Maybe that was the thing burning a hole in his gut. He lived to work, to take down bad guys, and Pierce and he had been casing the Triple B for months now, hoping to hit on what they considered an illegal ring that dealt in drugs and gun smuggling. Among other things.

Cataloging all of his rationalizations for later—much later—he went to her. "Are you okay?"

Emma turned to him, her eyes a misty blue-green washed in dusk. "No, I'm not okay. Someone was killed because of me."

"Possibly," he said, wishing he hadn't blurted that out to her. He'd planned on telling her later after they'd had time to talk. But she seemed to hit all his hot buttons. "We don't know for sure yet if Junior's death is related to what happened to you."

"But it looks that way, doesn't it?"

"Yes."

It all added up. The kid had tried to help Ryder and someone had snitched to Bounce and Ounce. Too much of a coincidence to think of it any other way.

"It happens," he said. "Junior had a hard life, but he chose to stay on the streets."

"I'm so sorry, Ryder. I think it is my fault and I don't know what else to say. None of you are safe with me here."

He didn't touch her. But he wanted to. Too soon, way too crazy for his brain to comprehend. "If you really want to leave, I'll find a safe house for you and put a detail on you."

Emma whirled, causing Spur to back up and woof. "I wanted to leave. Wanted to find a car and just drive. But

I don't have any cash or any information or even much of an identity, and you have my weapon. I feel safe here and I know I need to rest and get my head straight. But Ryder, something is eating at me. Something I can't explain. I think I'm holding back because I'm afraid of what I might remember. Something I don't want to or can't remember. I've never felt so helpless."

Ryder felt kind of helpless right now, too.

"How about we slow down and think this through. We'll start with what we know about you and what I know about the Triple B and compare notes and I'll keep digging on your clients and your family and anything else I can find. Something has to jog your memory. The doctor said this is temporary, so one day it should all fall into place."

She nodded and rubbed Spur's fuzzy head. "What if that one day takes a long time? I can't stay here forever."

He couldn't answer that even though forever with her might not be a bad thing. Scratching that as the worst idea ever, he said, "Look, I don't know. I promise I will do everything in my power to make that day come quick. But I need you to cooperate with me, not fight me at every turn."

She stared down at Spur and then glanced back at Ryder, her expression more settled, her eyes calm now. "I don't have much of a choice. You're the only person who can help me."

He smiled at that. "Not exactly what a man wants to hear but I'll take it."

Emma touched a hand to his arm. "Hey, if God is in the details, then He brought us together for a reason. I'm clinging to that as my first answer."

Touched that she still had faith, Ryder saw she meant it. He agreed. "God will see us through. He's helped me through a lot of tight spots." Then he winked at her. "And right now, I'm thanking Him for letting me cross your path. Not only because I want to help you but because…I like you. You're different."

"You have no idea," she said, turning back toward the house. Then with a wry grin, she added, "And neither do I, really."

Spur woofed at that and took the lead. As smitten as he was with Emma, the dog knew it was supper time.

But Ryder stopped her before they went back inside. "How did today go with my mom and sister?"

She crossed her arms and gave him a feminine smirk. "That's on a need-to-know basis, Detective."

"You know they'll try to throw us together, right?"

Her eyes flared to green. "Right. I figured that. But… hey, God's already taken care of that part by throwing us together in that alley. Doesn't mean anything will come of it."

"Technically, Pierce found you first. But you scare him, so I took the fall and agreed to be your bodyguard."

She balked at that, her pretty eyes flaring. "I don't need a bodyguard. I need a good detective."

"Why can't I be both?"

She gave him another on-fire glance. "Why don't we agree to be partners so we can find out what Bounce, Ounce and all the other lowlifes at the Triple B are up to?"

"Deal," he said, holding out his hand.

She took it and gave him a mighty firm handshake. "Deal."

Ryder felt better already. Better, but still cautious. He had to keep his head in the game. Bringing down the Triple B— that was his goal. Helping Emma was just a side effect of his work. He helped people all the time, both good and bad people.

But he was pretty sure she was one of the good ones. Somehow, being with Emma had turned a bad day into an okay day. She'd agreed to stay here where he prayed she'd be safe and she'd talked partner—work—just work. Nothing else, nothing more. He had to agree with that, too. He could breathe again and forget about that not-gonna-happen thing that he wanted to happen. But she seemed to still have that spark of spunk he liked.

Now he'd just have to tell his nosy dog to back off.

And his well-meaning but nosy family, too.

She was running down a dark alley. Someone called out to her. A face in the shadows. Footsteps pounded behind her. If she didn't get to the end of the alley, she'd die.

And she'd never know who was calling to her.

Then the pain. A great ripping pain.

Emma screamed and sat up in bed.

A dream. She'd had a bad dream.

A cold sweat made her shiver and hold the lightweight blanket close while her eyes adjusted to the shadows dancing through the moonlight that streamed in through the sheer curtains.

The door to her bedroom burst open and Ryder stood in sweatpants and a T-shirt, his gun pointed while he covered every corner of the room.

"Are you all right?" he asked before he flipped on the nearest table lamp.

She nodded, took in deep breath. "A dream. No, a nightmare."

She heard footsteps on the stairs. Ryder headed to the door to ward off his mother and sister. "She had a bad dream. She's okay. I got it."

Leaving the door ajar and the lamp on, he placed his gun on the desk by the window. "Want some water?"

She pointed to the bathroom. "I brought a glassful in here with me earlier."

He got the glass of water and handed it to her, then sat down in the chair beside the bed, his big frame overpowering the dainty slipper chair. "You have a good set of lungs."

Emma sipped the water and then rubbed her hand down her face. "It was so real."

He looked as rattled as she felt. His hair was mussed and his clothes rumpled. "Want to talk about it?"

She nodded. "Yes. Maybe I'll remember something."

After he took the water glass back and set it on the nightstand, she pushed at her hair and took a breath. "I was in an alley. Maybe the alley."

"You mean the one behind the Triple B?"

"Yes. Someone was calling out, screaming. I recognized the voice. I was running toward her."

"It was a female voice?"

She nodded, her hands clenched together. "Yes. She sounded so scared."

His gaze held steady on Emma, both helpful and distracting. "What else, Emma?"

"I don't know. I heard footsteps behind me and I couldn't run fast enough. She kept calling, screaming. She needed help."

Ryder leaned over and took her hand. "What happened next?"

"The pain. An intense pain. And then I woke up."

"You remembered the pain of being hit over the head?"

She looked into his eyes, tears blurring her vision. "No. I remembered the pain of my heart being ripped from my body." When he looked shocked, she added, "Not physically, Ryder. But…my heart hurt so much because it seemed broken. So broken." Then she put her hands to her face. "I think that's the sadness that's been pushing at me. That pain I can't bear to feel and that I don't want to remember. And that scares me way more than being hit with a baseball bat."

Ryder moved closer to take one of her hands again, his eyes a deep bronze. "Tomorrow, Emma. Tomorrow I'm staying home and we're going over all of it, okay? So you can find out what happened before you got to the Triple B. We'll put it all together to come up with whatever brought you there."

"I don't think I want to remember, but I have to know what's going on."

"Yes, you do. And no matter how bad it is, we'll handle it together."

She held his hand, thinking she wasn't the touchy-feely kind. She couldn't remember what kind she was, but she knew she didn't like people hovering. But this quiet, gentle handholding with a man who seemed to live up to his promises wasn't so bad. Ryder's hands were strong and tanned and calloused, rough in some places but soft in others. He had the kind of presence that made people feel secure and safe.

But she couldn't get used to this. She couldn't hold his hand and let him fix everything. That she knew. Emma handled her own messes. Or did she? Had she somehow messed everything up?

That distant panic hit her, so she pulled away and tugged the covers over her T-shirt. "I'm okay now. I'll be all right."

He nodded and stood but didn't look convinced. "You know I'm right across the hall."

"Yes." She was well aware of that. Too aware.

"Good night." He gave her one last once-over, retrieved his gun and then closed the door.

"Good night," she whispered after he'd left.

Without him, the room grew too big and too shadowy, making her imagine things that weren't there. Those unseen things that remained unexplainable. But she wasn't a coward. Emma turned off the lamp and let her eyes adjust to the darkness. But she didn't go back to sleep. Between 3:00 a.m. and dawn, she lay watching the windows and listening to the house creak, her mind still in that dream where the screams called out her name.

She hadn't told Ryder that part. That the person calling out had screamed Emma's name. "Emma, Emma, help me, Emma. Please."

Emma knew she wouldn't rest easy again if she didn't find who had been calling her for help.

What if that scared, desperate person was still out there somewhere, waiting for her to come and find her?

SEVEN

"Maybe you should call some of your former foster parents. That couple you saw in the photo Ryder found could be someone you were once close to or knew."

Emma looked up at Nancy and shook her head. She and Ryder had spent most of the day piecing together her past, with Nancy stepping in to help her with the memory loss and to make sure she didn't overtax herself. Emma was tired but refused to give up. The dream she'd had last night had left her rattled and having Ryder come to her rescue had left her unsettled. She didn't want to become attached to him, and she sure didn't want to depend on him. Feeling like an invalid made her only want to push further.

So why wasn't she jumping at the chance to find out about that couple in the photo?

Each time she looked at the photo lying on the table, Emma felt something akin to fear and dread in her heart and her stomach started roiling with what she knew must be some kind of anxiety. Did she have a built-in warning system?

"I don't know why I'm not sure about them, but I don't think I'm ready for that," Emma said, her gut burning again. But then, that connection might help her to remember and get on with what she came here to do.

Ryder's concentrated stare shifted from her to his mother. "I have my friend down there checking them out. Maybe after we hear from him Emma will be more inclined to approach them."

"Yes," she said, feeling better because he'd supported her decision. "Yes, that makes sense. I hope he won't mention me."

Ryder nodded. "He's good at pretexting, so I don't think that will be a problem."

Maybe she *should* contact the couple, but this was the safer way. Glancing at Nancy, she said, "After we hear from Ryder's source down in Houston. Then I'll decide on whether to contact them or not." Then she thought back over what they knew right now.

She had lived in several foster homes on the outskirts of Houston, but they'd have to go to the courthouse in that county and dig up the records to find out who had fostered her. Her school years seemed to have been uneventful other than being moved from foster home to foster home. Cheerleading, football games, the usual. But when she thought of her senior year, Emma got a sick kind of feeling inside her heart. What was she refusing to remember?

"I can't seem to conjure up any memory of what happened after my senior year. Talk about a real 'gap' year."

"This couple could fill in the missing gap," Ryder said. Tapping his pen on the tabletop, he pointed to the photo.

"You mean about the year I seem to have disappeared?"

"Well, I don't think you disappeared, but you went somewhere and I can't find any information on that one year and you can't seem to remember it."

Did he still think she was holding back? Well, she was. She couldn't bring up the memories. For someone who liked to control her own destiny, this was seriously driving her nuts.

Emma got up and paced in front of the window. Spur decided to join her. Something about that missing year brought out the sadness that threatened to break her heart. Where had she gone?

"Maybe I had amnesia that year, too."

"You seem to have blocked it," Nancy said, her tone gentle. "It happens with amnesia. It's sometimes called hysterical amnesia. When your mind just can't absorb what's happening. Or what happened. You knew it all, but the trauma to your head caused a shift and now you could be unconsciously blocking the worst of your memories or it could truly be from the head wound."

"So because I lost some of my marbles, I'm blocking the things I don't want to think about or remember?"

Nancy nodded. "A hypnotist might be able to help, but getting in touch with anyone from your past could trigger all of your memories, good or bad."

Emma watched Ryder. He didn't comment but he gave her a blank stare. "Mom, maybe Emma isn't close to this couple. Maybe she doesn't want them involved or maybe they're part of the reason she came here. Let's wait until we find out more."

Emma's pulse buzzed on that suggestion. "I don't remember but…it just feels wrong to call them right now. Let's go over my client list. Ryder, you said you dug around on that, right? Maybe they're my last clients and I'm dreading having to tell them I failed. We need to know more about my work records."

He nodded and grabbed his phone. "I'll give my guy another call and put some fire under him."

Emma turned from her pacing. "Tell whoever you hired to break into my files, if need be."

"I think he's doing that already," Ryder said with a

sheepish expression. "He's gifted at hacking into computer systems."

Ryder's phone buzzed before he could call his friend. "It's Pierce. He might have found something."

"Hey," he said into the phone. "I'm gonna put you on speaker. Just a sec." He gave his mother a warning glance. "Mom, do you mind?"

Nancy got up and held her hands up. "I have things to do out in the barn." Giving Emma a soft smile, she left them to it.

After his mother had called to Spur and shut the back door, he checked his watch. "Stephanie won't be home until later. We have the house to ourselves. Go ahead, Pierce. I have Emma here with me."

"All right." Pierce cleared his throat. "So we haven't found a phone or a rental car. Nor a car registered to your name, Miss Langston. I can't say how you got to the Triple B. We can check with DART surveillance videos for the last week to see if you boarded one of the train cars."

Emma nodded to Ryder. "I'd appreciate that."

Ryder spoke up. "Anything from the Dumpster?"

"Just a lot of fingerprints, and some of those belonged to Ounce. Of course, he probably takes out the trash every day, so to speak. But that does place him in the alley. We'll try on some of the other prints, too. Still waiting on the lab regarding the DNA samples we took."

After a pause, he added, "And we didn't find anything in the trash, and let me tell you, it had been sitting there a few days. I'm going to burn the clothes I had on yesterday."

"So we know Emma was at the bar and we have reason to believe that Bounce and Ounce took her out back to either work her over or kill her."

His gaze hit on Emma. "Sorry," he said, "we pretty

much know it was them, but it's the way things are until we have more evidence."

"I get it," she replied. "That much we can all agree on." Then she started pacing again. "No car keys, no phone, no purse. But they didn't get my wallet with my ID and badge."

"That's because I came along," Pierce said. "I think they would have taken your wallet and finished you off if they hadn't been interrupted."

"I'll be back in town tomorrow," Ryder said. "I'm going to send someone in to question everyone in the bar again. Just show them Emma's picture and see how they react and hope I rustle up a Bounce or an Ounce. They can't hide forever."

"And we stay undercover," Pierce said. "I dressed like a homeless man to go Dumpster diving, and besides, no one from the bar saw me. I have been surveilling the place but mostly just the usual crowd coming and going. No sign of Petey. I got nothing else. I'm sorry, Miss Langston."

"Call me Emma," she said, her head already hurting. "Who is Petey?"

"Petey Smith. The man we were going after when Pierce found you," Ryder explained. "We had an outstanding warrant on him, so we thought we'd take him in and get some answers to what goes on in that place."

"He's lying low," Pierce said. "Something is up for sure. I'm not gonna give up."

"I'll be back to help," Ryder said. "Meantime, I'm waiting on my friend from Houston to see what he's found regarding Emma's client list."

Emma leaned against the counter and looked at Ryder. "I could go back to the bar," she said.

"No," both Ryder and Pierce replied.

"Bad idea," Ryder told her.

"But maybe if I go back to the alley I can remember something else."

"Only as a last resort," Ryder said. "And only if we're with you."

Sensing a discussion he probably didn't want to be involved in, Pierce said, "I gotta go. You know, *my* work is never done." Then he chuckled. "Why is it you get to guard Miss Emma and I get all the grunt work?"

"Seniority," Ryder said before ending the call.

Emma sat staring up at him. "He does have a point. You don't have to guard me when you could be out there finding out the truth."

"You don't get it, do you?" he said. "The truth is right here between us. But it's locked inside your brain."

Ryder went about the few chores he still liked to do himself. He checked on the working horses and did the rounds in the pasture to make sure the fences were secure. Then he stopped to observe the herd of longhorns meandering in their slow, gangly way near the creek bed, his big roan, Bad Boy, knowing the trails better than he did.

Ryder had to get back to work tomorrow. Hanging around with Emma all day had been a bad idea. She stirred things inside him that he'd rather leave still. Things that made him think of family and this ranch and the quiet solitude of the end of a hard day's work. A solitude that included coming home to a woman he could love.

His mother tried on every level to set him up with nice women, but Ryder no longer fell for her well-meaning ploys. He'd come close once with one of his matchmaking mom's picks.

Mia.

She'd been intriguing and pretty, smart and sassy. On her way from college and being a sorority girl to starting a career in marketing. They'd met at one of the Palace bar-becues and his mother had beamed with pride when Ryder had asked Mia out on a date. One date led to another, but on what should have been a very important night, he'd been called into town on a pending case. He'd missed her big birthday party. That canceled date led to a big fight.

And so did the next one and the next one. Mia wanted him on her terms. Wanted him to be there when she had downtime and expected him to understand when her job became demanding. They both had busy careers, but hers was safe and high maintenance.

His was dangerous and full of evil.

Mia decided she'd had enough, had accused him of not having a soul. He'd agreed with that notion when he found her out on a date with a man who had money and knew when to get home to his woman.

Ryder hadn't even confronted her. He'd just told her they were done.

And that was that.

Now, being around Emma was the exact opposite of what he thought he'd felt for Mia. Mia had been safe and easy and a convenience. But Emma wasn't safe or easy, and she sure wasn't convenient. She had secrets and lost memo-ries. She obviously had a past that not even he could crack.

He couldn't trust what she knew or what she was hid-ing. And yet, he wanted to know all about her. Not just because of finding her in the middle of his undercover investigation either. More because since the minute he'd laid eyes on the woman, his heart had done funny little bumps and an electric current of awareness seemed to hum through his brain.

He'd thought going on a long ride around the ranch would clear his head, but no, he only had more questions. *No*, he told himself, *you don't want to mess with this situ-*

*ation. Let her find out the truth and help her, but let her
go when this is over.*

He didn't have room in his heart for a love affair. He'd
been on the fast track to find criminals for so long now,
Ryder wondered if he hadn't lost part of his soul.

His mother prayed for him.

His sister teased him.

His partner worried about him.

But Emma, she just stared him down and turned his
questions around on him. He couldn't have a woman with
that kind of sharpness shining a light into his rotten soul.
He was fearless on the streets but a coward when it came
to confronting his own shortcomings. He wouldn't expose
himself to that kind of scrutiny again.

Now, he let Bad Boy gallop toward home and decided
he'd play it cool from here on out with Emma. He couldn't
keep her. It was that simple. And the sooner she regained
her memory, the better. He might have to call that couple
in the picture himself, whether she liked it or not, to see
if he could get things rolling.

But when he reached the pasture behind the house and
looked up to find Emma there waiting at the fence, her
gaze on him, her hair glistening a burnished russet in the
gloaming, Ryder's heart got the best of his head.

He could certainly appreciate coming home to her every
night. But what if she, like Mia, decided she couldn't handle what he did for a living? And what if, like Mia, Emma
chose to walk away and back to her own life instead of
choosing him? What if that happened? Then what would
he do?

He and Mia were never meant for each other.

But Emma? She seemed to fit into his world in a way
that worried him and enticed him. Only he was too much
of a coward to accept that right now.

Even when she stood there looking at him with those incredible eyes and that forlorn, uncertain expression on her face.

Ryder geared up to go back to being a hard-nosed vice cop, his speech prepared.

But just as he trotted Bad Boy up to the fence so he could talk to her, a shot rang out over the night. Followed by several more.

EIGHT

Ryder sent his horse running to the barn and then dived over the fence and pushed Emma to the ground. Holding her there, he looked toward where the shots had come from—a copse of trees near the edge of the small creek.

He could hear Spur barking inside the house and prayed his mom wouldn't let the dog out. Horses whinnied and kicked inside the barn, and the few heads of cattle grazing nearby dashed away.

"Are you all right?" he asked Emma, still holding her down.

"I'm okay. How many?" she asked. When she lifted her head an inch, more shots shattered the air.

"Not sure," he replied, pushing her down again, his breath coming in huffs. "We need to get to the barn."

"Do you have a weapon?"

"Yeah. But a handgun won't help when we've got a sniper on our tail. We need someone to cover us." He looked at the trees again, then pulled out his cell and sent an alert text to all available personnel and to his mother and sister, something they used on the ranch all the time to warn of dangers such as fire or hurt animals or humans. Didn't use it much for human intruders.

SHOOTERS IN TREES BY THE POND. COMING FROM
THE WEST. NEED COVER.

Ryder glanced toward the barn and saw rifles peeking out of windows and doors. Then he moved his head
slightly toward the house. Spur had quieted and a curtain
was pulled back in an upstairs window.

Lowering his head, he ignored the floral scent wafting
from Emma's hair and whispered in her ear. "When I say
go, I want you to run toward the barn, toward the doors.
Someone will let you inside."

"What about you?"

"I'm going to cover you, along with my men inside
who are waiting."

"Are you sure this will work?"

"If you run fast, yes." He looked into her eyes, his heart
beating against hers. "Belly-crawl if you have to and don't
look back."

She nodded and gave him a solid stare. "Be careful,
Ryder."

Another shot hit the air.

"Just do it, Emma."

He signaled to the barn, then did a roll away from her.
"Go."

Emma lifted into a crouch and scooted to the barn. The
door flew open and an arm dragged her inside, bullets hitting wood and stone all around her.

Ryder recovered and found shelter behind a big stone
flowerpot. A shot whizzed by, cracking the pot.

Then came return fire from the barn and the house.

He lifted his Glock and emptied several rounds out of
the magazine, knowing he'd never hit the shooter from this
far. But all the return fire paid off. The shooter went silent.

Waving a hand for his men to stand down, Ryder waited a couple of beats. Had some of their bullets hit the shooter?

Ryder lifted and hurried through the unlocked gate, his gun aimed at the trees. Out in the open pasture now, he stood still and watched the woods. A lone figure appeared, his rifle trained on Ryder.

Ryder called out, "Don't move." The rifleman kept coming and took another shot, aimed at Ryder. Ryder dived to the ground, the bullet just missing him. He shot back and missed. The man kept coming. A volley hit from behind Ryder, but the bullets from his men could go only so far.

Ryder knew he'd never make it through the gate. He had nowhere to hide. The man took aim, ignoring the danger.

Then he heard a crash from the barn followed by one shot.

The man coming for him flinched, dropped his rifle and then clutched a hand to the blood pouring out of his chest.

He hit the ground with a grunt and a thud. He didn't move again.

Everything went quiet. And then everything came alive again, shouts and footsteps hitting dirt, doors opening and people talking.

Ryder glanced around and looked up at the house. His mother cracked the back door open and waved. "We're okay."

Then he looked toward the barn. No rifles poking out the lower-level windows. Most everyone who'd been working came running. One of his men peeked out of the barn door and pointed up.

Ryder glanced toward the small window up in the loft.

A pane had been broken out...and Emma stood inside at the window, holding what looked like a long-range rifle with an impressive scope.

She'd saved his life.

* * *

"That woman knows her way around a rifle."

Ryder nodded to his ranch foreman and turned to find the woman whom tight-lipped, ornery Jack Murphy had just praised. "You can say that again."

The ranch was now teeming with sheriff's deputies and a couple of techs from Ryder's division of the Dallas/Fort Worth police station. He'd have to give a thorough report to the chief first thing tomorrow.

The man in the woods was now dead from a single shot straight to the chest. And he'd been identified as Petey Smith.

They could mark him off their list but whoever was after Emma had to have sent him.

Emma sat with his mother on a big sectional near the pool, watching as crime scene techs and sheriff's deputies roamed around the pasture and yard. Ryder couldn't decide whether she was as cool as a cucumber or if she was in shock.

He nodded to Pierce, glad the kid had taken point. He was too tired to argue with anybody.

Pierce rushed by. "I want a promotion."

"Oh, I think you'll get one."

Ryder headed toward his mother and Emma. Stephanie came out, carrying a tray that contained iced tea and cookies. They'd already put out water, tea and coffee for the investigators.

"How we doing?" Ryder asked as he sank down across from the women, his eyes on Emma.

His mother gave him an unsure shrug. "I think we're okay."

Emma glanced back at the woods and then over to Ryder. "I… I've never shot a person before."

"He was trespassing and he opened fire on my land and

my people. He had me cornered and you took care of him. You did what you had to do."

"Are you sure Emma's shot killed the man?" Stephanie asked, awe in her words. "I heard all kinds of shooting."

"Pretty sure," Ryder replied, his eye still on Emma. "Only a person with a scoped rifle could have made that shot. Someone who's experienced with guns."

She was quiet. Too quiet. Had she recognized Petey and killed him because she knew he'd kill her? Or because he knew who she was and could expose her?

Would he ever be able to trust her?

Well, she had saved his life. That had to count for something. Right now, he needed to make sure she was okay, get her someone who could help her through this.

The church pastor was good at this. He'd call him. The man had helped Ryder deal with a lot of horrible things. Maybe he could help Emma, too.

His mother poured freshly brewed tea over clinking ice and then set the pitcher down and took a couple of sips of hers. "I guess I'd better finish dinner. We still need to eat. Stephanie, I need you in the kitchen."

"What?" Stephanie's eyebrows did a perfect V slant. "I just got out here."

"And you'll just go back inside with me," Nancy said, giving her daughter a warning glare.

Stephanie tossed her hair and flipped her flip-flops a little too loudly.

Ryder got up and poured himself some tea and then sat down next to Emma. "Did you know Petey Smith?"

"No," she said. "I've already told everyone that. I gave a full report. I think I'm clear since I shot him to keep him from killing you."

"Yes, and you had witnesses to attest to that, but we

still have to go through the routine of questioning people in a homicide."

"Am I going to jail?"

"Not if I can help it."

She put her head in her hands. "I can't believe this is happening. I need to be out there, searching, and now I've got this hanging over my head."

"I think you'll be cleared but…you might get a whole lot more questions before this is over."

"So I killed the man you wanted to bring in."

"Yes." When she didn't speak, he said, "Emma, talk to me."

She stared over at him, her eyes holding that green mist. "I killed a man, Ryder. And I don't know why he was here, but you were out there earlier riding your horse and he didn't shoot you. But he wanted me dead and then he was coming for you and I had to do something. I didn't think. I just reacted."

Ryder scooted closer. "Jack said you went straight to the gun cabinet that he'd unlocked and found the rifle, loaded it with the proper ammo and headed upstairs. Do you remember doing that?"

Giving him a scrutinizing stare, she said, "Yes, of course I can remember. I asked for a weapon early on and then I headed upstairs to see if there was a window I could use. When I realized you were trapped, I got into position, got a bead on the shooter and waited for the perfect shot. I thought I'd just hit him, bring him down. I… I wasn't trying to kill him. Until he started coming for you with a loaded weapon."

She stood and paced. "I've never seen him before. But he obviously found his way onto your land."

"Yeah, and I'm not happy about that. I'll post guards into the far woods for the duration of your stay."

"That might not be long. I can't do this. I won't put your family at risk any longer."

Ryder leaned in, his hand on her arm. "And I won't let you go out there and fight this thing by yourself. I mean it, Emma. If you go now, it won't matter. We're all involved. And I can't help you if I can't find you."

Ryder's cell phone buzzed. "It's my buddy from Houston," he said, standing. "Let's go inside so we can have some privacy."

Emma nodded, glanced toward the small spot of trees where the shooter had died and then turned and headed for the house.

Ryder hoped his man had found something they could work with. He didn't know how long he could keep protecting a woman who seemed bound and determined to do things her way.

A woman who was obviously trained to take care of herself, at that.

Emma followed Ryder upstairs and into a small office that had a view of the backyard and the pasture beyond.

He pointed to a small plaid sofa and she sat down, her mind still reeling from what had happened earlier. She'd have nightmares about shooting that man.

"Are you ready?" he asked, his hand over his cell phone.

She nodded and took a breath.

"Hey, Chad, I have Emma Langston with me. I'm putting you on speaker so she can hear what you have to say."

"Hi, Chad," Emma said, her tone stronger than she felt. Her hands were sweaty and she thought she might hyperventilate. What was wrong with her?

"Hello," Chad said, his voice sure and steady. "Well, I've got some information and I hope it helps. First, I was able to get into your files. Might want to beef up your electronic security. You are one busy person, Miss Langston. You deal mostly with missing people and…finding adopted children for their birth parents."

Emma's heart did that skip, skip, skip followed by bump, bump, bump. She was fighting against this. She could feel it in her whole being. But she was also still in shock from shooting another human being. Had she done that before? "Go on," she said.

Ryder shot her a worried glance and then came and sat down beside her, the phone with him. "What did you find, Chad?"

"The people in the photo are your last known clients, Joseph and Annette Parker. You received a call from them about a week ago, according to the phone records I found." He gave her the date and time.

Emma's skin singed with a cold sweat. She blinked, prayed, wished she could disappear. Parker. She knew that name as well as she knew her own. And she knew who they were.

The Parkers. The couple in the picture Ryder had found in her wallet.

The memories started boiling over like hot water. She grabbed Ryder's hand, tears blurring her eyes. "They needed my help, right? They needed me to help them."

"Yes, ma'am. They asked you to find their missing daughter, Reese."

Emma let go of Ryder and stood, every emotion she'd ever lived rushing through her like a raging river. The pain she'd felt since she'd woken up in the hospital gripped her and cut off her breath. Now she understood why she'd fought against remembering even when she needed to be out there, searching. Because she'd failed, because it might be too late and she couldn't bear to think about that. Or what that could mean for the Parkers and for her.

She whirled. "I know what I need to do now. I have to go. I have to find her."

Ryder grabbed her and held her. "Chad, I'll call you back. She's remembering…all of it."

He ended the call and pulled Emma close. "What is it? Why do you need to go right now?"

She gulped and grabbed his shirt, her hands cold, her body trembling. She wanted to hold tight to him. Just hold tight. But she couldn't do that.

Instead, she looked into his eyes and with tears running down her face, she told Ryder the truth. "I have to find Reese Parker. I have to find her because she's my daughter."

NINE

Ryder sat her down and held her hand, his expression bordering on shock. "You're gonna need to explain this to me."

Emma wiped at her eyes, her memories crashing against reality while shock made her numb with fear. "I can't sit here and explain, Ryder. I have to find her. It's been almost a week now."

"I get that," he said. "And now that we know you're definitely looking for a young girl who went missing, we can start there."

"You don't get it," Emma said, getting up again. "Not just any young girl. My biological daughter, Ryder. I have to go back to the Triple B. They could have her there."

Ryder took a long breath and stood between her and the door. "We're going to find her, Emma. But I need to hear what you remembered first." Then because he must have sensed how much she wanted to go, just go, he added, "I'm going to send an alert to the Dallas Police Department once you give me details. She'll go on the missing teen list immediately. In fact, she should already be on it."

"But I didn't see her in the photos you showed me."

Holding Emma's arms, he said, "The first step is to relax and give me all the information you can remember."

Emma wanted to rush past him but knew it would be

foolish. So she sat back down in the chair across from his desk.

"Her name is Reese Parker. She's fifteen. The Parkers are good parents. They dote on her and, well, I guess, spoil her. They live in a swanky neighborhood on the outskirts of Dallas."

"What? But that address on the back of the photo was for a location near Houston."

"I know," Emma said, calmer now. "That's the address of where they lived when I first found them over five years ago. They moved here for Mr. Parker's work but we kept in touch even though they had moved again just recently, into a more private neighborhood. She'd started at a new school a couple of months ago. A private school and one of the best in the area where they live."

Holding her hands together, she said, "I can't believe I'm remembering all of this. How could I forget something so important?"

She tried to get her memories cataloged, but her mind was still on GO mode, everything tumbling and hitting against her brain in brilliant colors. But her past was right there, stamped in her head, even the memories she'd tried to repress.

"Just take your time," Ryder said, his eyes dark with empathy and concern. "So you gave her up when you were around sixteen?"

"Yes," Emma said, that sickly feeling hitting her stomach. "I met a boy at school when I was in my last foster home. He was older than me, a football player, popular, and he lived next door. I had such a crush on him and… he took advantage of that." Closing her eyes, she bit back at the trauma, the horror of what he'd done. "He told me he loved me, would always love me. That we'd be together forever. But he only wanted a few minutes with me, really."

Ryder lowered his head. "He got you pregnant."

She nodded, the shame still as sharp as ever, tears burning at her eyes. "I had to give up my baby, Ryder. I didn't have any choice. The boy ignored me after a couple of dates, then he graduated and headed out for a summer job and on to college. I thought he'd come back for me like he promised when we were together, but he didn't. I never told him I was pregnant. He wouldn't have cared." She stopped, took in air. "He died in a horrible car wreck a month later. I knew I couldn't give a child a good life, not in the shape I was in and with no hope or no income. I did it for her."

Ryder lifted his head, his eyes holding regret. "I'm sorry, Emma. For what happened to you and for what you had to give up. It makes sense now, that push-pull of you wanting to get back out there but being afraid to give in to your memories."

Those horrible memories, followed by the anguish of having to give up her baby, tore through Emma like a jagged piece of barbed wire. She couldn't handle his sympathy or the pain she saw in Ryder's eyes. He couldn't see that her whole life had been shaped by one horrible mistake. A mistake that had brought her a beautiful daughter she couldn't keep. No wonder she didn't date much. Her trust in men had ended when the boy had left without her. Left her there all alone and afraid. Her pain had been even worse when she'd heard he'd been killed in that crash. Drunken driving. She'd mourned him and she'd mourned what had happened between them. But she couldn't regret giving birth to Reese. Up until a few days ago, Reese had lived a good life.

Why? Emma had to wonder why this had happened to such a sweet family.

She'd vowed she'd never feel that vulnerable again. But now, she felt more vulnerable than ever. Helpless.

She didn't plan on dating Ryder, so none of that mattered anyway. What mattered right now was finding Reese, and since Ryder had tried to help her, he deserved the truth.

She took a long breath and gathered her thoughts, placing them in order while she ignored the parts that were still blurred.

"When I turned eighteen and aged out, I decided from then on my life would be my own. So I got a job and managed to get into a community college. I studied criminal investigations, and after I graduated, I joined the local police academy and worked as a patrol officer in a small town down below Houston. But what I really wanted was to become a private investigator. So I could help people find other people, mostly. And because I wanted to find my daughter, just to make sure she was okay."

"So you quit the police department?"

"Yes, but only after I met a man who was a PI, an older fellow named Wade Johnson. He was a real family man and he and his wife, Becky, took me under their wing. Becky ran the office and kept us on our toes, but they taught me so much about life."

Ryder smiled at that. "Probably just what you needed."

"Yes." Those memories were wonderful. "We had worked some cases together since he crossed paths with the police a lot, and about three years after I'd worked day and night and hadn't moved up the ladder at the police station, he came to me and offered me a job with him. I trusted Wade, so I said yes. He trained me on everything from weapons to self-defense. In my downtime, I searched adoption records and snooped around in foster care records until I finally found the Parkers. They had adopted my baby girl. I got in touch with them and assured them

I didn't want Reese to know about me unless they agreed and only if she was ready. I just wanted to know she was safe and happy."

She stopped, tears streaming down her face, her gaze on Ryder. "And she was happy and healthy and doing great in school and…so beautiful. I didn't want to disrupt her life."

Ryder kneeled down in front of her. "You did the best you could for her, Emma. And now, you're gonna have to do that again. The best you can for your daughter. We will find her. I promise you that."

His assurances gave Emma the strength she needed. Now her whole life was there, right back where it needed to be, the good and the bad. But the urgency that had brought her here remained front and center.

"I have to find her, Ryder." She shook her head. "I had a picture of her, so I could ask around. You didn't find that in my wallet?"

"No," he said. "Did you have it that night at the Triple B?"

"I think so," she said. "I can't remember but it makes sense that I would have shown someone her picture."

"If you did and Bounce and Ounce saw you and recognized her, they would have taken the picture."

Emma's stomach roiled with apprehension and fear. "I can't think about that. If they took her, I will make them pay."

He pulled back but kept his hands on her arms. "Do you know what happened when she went missing? Did she run away?"

Emma shook her head. "She didn't run away. I verified that. She was with friends at a coffee shop in a strip mall near where the Parkers live. The girls had all walked there together, but her two friends had to leave early. A parent picked them up to head into the city, so Reese told them she'd walk home. It was only a few blocks away from the gate to the neighborhood. But Reese never made it home. They called the local sheriff, and then when things stalled out the Parkers became frantic. They called me."

Ryder frowned. "If they called the locals, why didn't she show up when I did a search?"

Emma thought about that. "They live just over the county line, so the local sheriff took over, but as I said, according to the Parkers, they didn't get in a big hurry about things. They assured Mr. and Mrs. Parker that they'd sent the alert but who knows. They didn't seem very cooperative and seemed to think Reese was a runaway."

"Or maybe we didn't go back far enough," Ryder said, already tapping on his phone. "I'm alerting everyone, statewide. Meantime, we need to call the Parkers and let them know what happened. And we'll need a new picture of Reese."

"Wow, that's some amazing story."

Ryder agreed with Pierce Daughtry. They were both back at the station today. Emma was in a small conference room, going through mug shots and photos they'd managed to snap while surveilling the Triple B, so she could possibly ID Bounce and Ounce. Now that Reese's picture was being broadcast to the whole state and beyond, volunteer organizations would help, too. Ryder and Pierce had to wait and see while they kept pounding the pavement and looking into any tips or leads. They'd put undercover people on the Triple B, with photos coming in here and there. Something had to give soon.

Ryder worried about Emma. She'd talked about her past a lot last night, telling Ryder and his mother what she'd remembered. Too hyper, too keyed up. She wanted to get

back to the city and start where she'd left off. That and her
anxiety over the shooting yesterday had him on full alert.

Nancy had convinced her to go to bed around midnight, but Ryder felt sure she hadn't slept much. He sure
hadn't either.

This morning, she'd been up and waiting with coffee,
fully dressed and ready to roll. He brought her into the
station for questioning and a by-the-book statement, but
he knew she was champing at the bit to get back out there.

"Yep. Emma has proof that she's the girl's biological
mother and she's been in touch with the adoptive parents.
She called the Parkers last night and told them what happened. They'd tried calling her but her phone went to the
not-available message. They wanted to come into the city,
but we talked them into staying at home since they could
still receive a ransom call."

"Too far out for that," Pierce said, shaking his head.
"You realize we might be too late on this one, right?"

Ryder didn't need that reminder. "Yes, but we aren't
going to voice that, okay? We presume she's alive until
we know she's not."

Pierce gave him a questioning glance. "Sure, okay."
Then he said, "What about this Wade guy? Does he know
Emma is here?"

"Wade died three years ago and his wife, Becky, is
with their son and family in Arizona," Ryder said. Just
one of the many details Emma had remembered. "Becky
sold the business to Emma. She's on her own with this investigation."

Ryder didn't want to think about what Emma would
do if they found the girl dead. Not a good scene. Since
she'd regained her memory full force after having shot a
man, Emma hadn't slept and she'd barely eaten anything.

She was hotwired for action, but he was trying to do this by the book so they wouldn't make any stupid mistakes.

Ryder rubbed his forehead. "I've got two men riding the fence line on the back of our property. Hopefully no one will get to her again."

"So where do we come in?" Pierce asked. "I mean, did the DA clear us to pursue this missing person case?"

"I'm waiting to hear, but it looks like a go," Ryder said. He'd had to do some tall talking to convince the district attorney and the prosecutor assigned to go after the Triple B that, yes, this girl's disappearance could help them bring down the Triple B. When he'd filed the entire report, including Emma's memory loss and recovery, everyone had taken notice.

Now if he could just focus on the investigation and not the woman at the center of things, he might make it through to the end.

Emma was a major distraction, and Ryder did not like distractions. He prided himself on being focused and on point.

This was a roller coaster of a ride that took him to new highs whenever Emma entered a room and new lows whenever he thought about getting involved with this beautiful, conflicted, determined woman. Not a good idea. She had "back off" written all over her, and for good reason. She'd been hurt both emotionally and physically, and some scars never healed.

So, why did the thought of having Emma in his life once the fires were put out keep popping into his head?

"Hey, Earth to Mr. Wonderful. Where do we go from here?"

Ryder sat up in his chair, his boots hitting the floor. "Well, since the locals bumbled the whole thing, we get dibs on this one. I don't think the locals will even care that much. When I called this morning, no one seemed to have any new information on the case. They were not happy that the Parkers had brought in a PI. Something is off with that sheriff's department and since they're in another county and under-manned, it's hard to pin them down on anything."

"Think they're hiding something?"

"I don't know yet," Ryder said. "But to drag your feet when a teenager is clearly missing. How does that make sense?"

"That is odd but, you know, maybe not enough manpower and lack of evidence or no leads."

Ryder stood and studied the whiteboard they'd put together starting with the timeline from the day Reese Parker had gone missing up until the night they'd found Emma and beyond. "*We* have evidence and *we* have manpower, but we need to connect this to our case, so I'm gonna look into why the authorities out at the Wood Hills substation have gone soft on this. For now, we have Emma at the Triple B, you found fingerprints that match one of the two men you saw that night and we had one witness who saw them stalking Emma."

"But a dead witness isn't very credible," Pierce reminded him. "Junior never stood a chance, did he?"

"No, and it's my fault," Ryder said. "I should have been more careful with him."

"Hey, he knew the risks, and he signed all the proper forms to be a CI, man. You can't take on everything that goes wrong, you know. Confidential informants live dangerous lives."

Ryder smiled at his buddy. "It's hard not to feel bad since I talked Junior into signing on the dotted line."

"Are you okay with all of this?" Pierce asked, his green

eyes studying Ryder while his grin held on. "You seem distracted."

"Why wouldn't I be distracted?" Ryder quipped. "We have a missing girl from a fairly wealthy family, a good-looking woman who is as tough as nails and an investigation into a notorious juke joint that we can't seem to crack. I have the DA and a prosecutor who wants to be the next DA breathing down my throat, and an obnoxious businessman who just wants to buy up property for his own private renaissance getting in my way, and I've got Petey Smith in the morgue right alongside Junior. Not to mention the FBI has us on their radar, too. What's not to love?"

Pierce lifted an eyebrow. "That good-looking woman—that's the part I'm worried about because she seems to be getting under your skin. You avoid women like the plague."

"I don't avoid women," Ryder said, frowning. "I happen to like women. They don't like me back. They think I'm too rough around the edges, broken, burned out, moody, hollow as a rotten log. And they don't like my line of work."

"Are you stating that as fact or quoting one of the many women you've left behind?"

"Quoting," Ryder admitted. "And sometimes they hurl explicit adjectives while they sling a shoe or two at me."

"This one that you mentioned, the tough-as-nails one," Pierce said, eying the doorway, "she's different, Ryder. You might want to watch your heart on her." Then he stood. "Oh, and by the way, she's standing at the door staring holes into your brawny back."

Ryder whirled away from the whiteboard and sure enough, Emma stood there leaning against the doorjamb, impatience scattered across her face like reckless freckles. "What's the holdup, Palladin? How many times do I need to tell you, I need to get out there and find Reese Parker."

TEN

"So we've widened the search," Ryder told her as they drove through the city. "I have this lead, but Emma, you have to understand that I shouldn't even have you with me. So you have to stay in the car and wait, okay?"

"Okay."

He wasn't convinced but he played along. "We'll try to nail down the man you found from looking at mug shots today. That's a start, your remembering him being at the Triple B that night."

"Yes, the face was familiar," she said, her eyes on the buildings and landscape whirling by. "But he wasn't with the two who cornered me in that alley."

"Nope, but at least you were able to identify them as Bounce and Ounce, and we have their given names, too. Now we're getting somewhere."

"Are we?" she asked, twisting around to glare at him. "No one seems to know where Bounce and Ounce are these days. I need to go back to the bar."

"No. We've had this discussion. They know you're alive and they've sent people after you. You're a material witness now, Emma. You saw their faces and you lived to tell about it. And you killed the hit man they sent to the ranch. They've gone to ground or they're on their way to

Mexico. But you don't need to go asking about them. And you shouldn't be with me either. Pierce is starting to get jealous of me spending time with you."

Emma hit the dashboard. "I can't take this helpless feeling. I feel like I need to be beating the bushes more."

"That's why I let you ride along." Ryder decided to distract her. "You never said how you traced Reese to the Triple B. Wanna tell me about that?"

She squinted into the late afternoon sunshine. "I drove to the big subdivision where the Parkers live and got a room nearby. Then I went straight to their house to gather information."

"We verified that hotel room since you remembered. But then you moved to another room in the city. Nothing odd in the second hotel room except that you'd booked it indefinitely."

She looked down at her jeans. "Yes, I have my suitcase back."

"No phone and nothing to indicate what you were up to."

"I always travel light."

"So what did you do once you'd talked to the Parkers?"

"I went to Reese's school and asked around. Talked to her teachers and friends, but some of her friends didn't want to chat with me. Nothing out of the ordinary there, but I did give them my number in case any of them remembered something—or wanted to tell me the truth. No teacher crushes or anything like that. No weird secret friends, based on her social media posts. The school had even set up a volunteer board to help search for her later that week."

She rubbed her head. "I'm remembering a lot but it comes in bits and pieces. I was so frantic when the Parkers called me for help, I don't even remember packing or booking any hotel room. I must have just picked one and found a place to toss my stuff until morning."

"But you are remembering details as they come, so that's good."

"Lots of details. I know her cell phone was missing because the Parkers had of course tried calling when she first went missing. The calls didn't go through."

"Okay, so…"

"I saw the Parkers and got what I could out of them and promised them I'd report back soon. By then it was well past midnight and I went back to my room and tried to jot down details. Then the next morning after I'd talked to some people at the school, I went to the strip mall where Reese disappeared. I identified myself to the coffee shop manager and showed him her picture."

She stopped, took in a breath. "She's a beautiful girl."

Ryder could feel the palpable pain radiating off her, but he knew tough could break if you picked at it too much. So he let her talk, wishing he could do more.

"I guess she got that from you," he said and then instantly regretted it. "I'm sorry."

"It's okay. We do have the same hair color, but her eyes are more hazel."

Ryder moved away from the personal stuff. "What did you learn from the manager?"

"He recognized her right away and seemed distraught that she was still missing a week after the incident."

"So he remembered that day?"

"He was working the afternoon when she left by herself, but he didn't think anything of it since kids walked to the coffee shop from the Wood Hills subdivision all the time."

"Do you have reason to suspect the manager?"

"No. He checked out clean."

"So then what?"

"I drove around to acclimate myself with the area and then I went back to the coffee shop and talked to the workers who were on the afternoon shift that day. They remembered her being with friends but the two friends had to leave early. Reese paid for her coffee, and told the worker she was walking home. None of them remembered anyone else being there, no one with her or stalking her. I got the owner of the strip mall to let me look at video surveillance for that week. I… I saw Reese with the girls and saw her leaving. Then I noticed a battered blue truck parked by the coffee shop. It backed out when Reese walked to the sidewalk into the subdivision."

"Did the truck follow her?"

"I don't know. The surveillance only showed the truck and Reese both near the exit from the property. A narrow sidewalk led into the gate of the subdivision. The gate is open during the day. Or at least it was that day." She grew quiet again. Ryder heard her swallow and saw her take in another breath. "That's the last anyone saw of her."

Ryder wanted to stop the car and sit and talk with her, but that wouldn't work for either of them right now. He wasn't sure he knew how to talk to a woman, really. He was more used to grilling hard-edged criminals. "You got a license plate off the truck?"

"Yes, that was easy, but I obviously didn't get to run the plate. I can give you the tag number."

"Okay, write it down and I'll call it in."

She took the pen and pad she'd brought along and jotted down the license plate letters and numbers.

"You must have had a good memory for details, before," Ryder noted. "You remembered the license plate."

"I'm a details person," she said. "Or at least I was."

"Your brain seems to be at top speed now."

Emma gave him a distracted glare. "I noticed something else on the truck's bumper."

"Yeah, what?"

"A bumper sticker. It had a bull's head on it and said,
'Blue Bull Bar. Stampeding in Downtown Dallas.'"

Emma grabbed his arm, the warm touch of her hand on
his bare skin sending a shock wave through his system.
"That's how I found the Triple B, Ryder."

She'd done everything right while the locals had done
everything wrong. They should have noticed that dark
blue pickup right away, but they probably didn't even ask
for surveillance tapes. If they had, they would have run
the plates through the system and put out an immediate
BOLO alert. Why had they stalled out on this case? Ryder
had put out feelers on that but the good-ole-boy network
wasn't responding so much.

Ryder had to admire her thoroughness. "So you decided
to check out the Triple B, based on seeing that sticker?"

"I immediately looked it up on my phone," she said, the
words rushed now. "Then I drove downtown and booked
that second room."

That seemed impulsive to Ryder, but then, he was learn-
ing that Emma had a reckless, impulsive nature.

"How did you get to the bar?"

"I called a cab," she said, surprise covering her face. "I
remember, Ryder. I called a cab and paid cash so no one
could trace me."

"That explains why we never found a car nearby."

"And why I was only carrying my wallet, my weapon
and my phone. I wanted to get in and get out, but I was
hoping I'd find the man with the truck."

Ryder sent her a quick glance, disapproval clouding his
judgment. "So you're saying you went there on a hunch,
not because you thought Reese could be there?"

"I went there because someone driving a truck with that bumper sticker could have possibly followed Reese or taken her. It was the only lead I had, but I did my research before I went to the Triple B. I read all the good and bad of it, pulled up some newspaper articles. My gut told me that if Reese had been taken there, I might not ever find her. But I had to start somewhere. I had to try. And…my gut is telling me that same thing now."

"Yeah, because they saw you and decided to stop you from doing anything else. So you're on the right track, Emma. And that is a very dangerous place to be right now. Exactly how many people did you talk to that night?"

"I don't remember. The place wasn't busy. Your friend Junior nodded to me. I remember that after seeing his mug shot. And I talked to a waitress and showed her Reese's picture. When I didn't get much of a response and everyone started avoiding me, I went outside to look for the truck."

She let out a gasp then. "I remember that, too. The truck was there that night, parked just off the alley near a wall. I was walking up to it when I heard the back door of the bar open. I turned to find Bounce and Ounce coming toward me. I never made it to the truck and I never figured out who was driving it."

Ryder filled in the rest. "So maybe the man you recognized in the mug shots today is the man who was driving that truck?"

"Yes," she said, smiling for the first time that day. "Yes." But then the smile ended. "He might be the man who took my daughter."

"Which means you're not staying in the car, right?"

"No, I am certainly not staying in the car. You said we'd do this together. I'm talking to this man and I'm going to find out what he knows."

* * *

Emma followed Ryder into the seedy-looking apartment complex. "How far are we from the Triple B?"

"About two blocks," Ryder said on a low whisper. "Remember, let me do the talking."

"Right." She really wanted to get to that bar, but if she walked in there and announced who she was and why she was there, Emma knew she'd be a dead woman.

"And this is just a fact-finding mission, okay?" Ryder said. "Don't let on about anything."

"Sure. Whatever."

"I mean it, Emma."

"I know you mean it, Ryder. Let's just get on with things."

"You're gonna be the death of me."

"Not if I can help it."

She didn't want him to get killed. She kind of liked him. But right now was not the time to explore the way he made her hair stand on edge or her heart do cartwheels. She knew the rules. A vice cop wouldn't want to come home to a private investigator. People like Ryder and she took their work home with them and carried it right on into their nightmares. Not exactly domestic tranquility.

Besides, she'd decided she never wanted to be involved with anyone. Growing up in the foster care system had caused Emma to distance herself from any lasting relationship. Better to leave first and not get hurt. Better to keep your heart close and always be on full alert. She hadn't been on alert when she was young and naive. Now she was searching for the child she'd had to give up.

"There." Ryder pointed to a corner apartment where a dead fern leaned like a sideways skeleton in a cracked pot on the stoop.

Emma followed him, both of them staying close to the

buildings. The air held a rancid smell that made Emma think of grease and dishwashing detergent. The late afternoon heat sliced with a razor-sharp precision through the alleyways between the crumbling brick buildings.

"A real resort, Palladin," she said, her mood as heated and conflicted as this desolate place.

"Yeah, well, welcome to the inner city, darlin'."

The way he said *darlin'* danced down her spine with glee.

Focus, Emma reminded herself, that gut-wrenching image of Reese walking away causing her to take in a gulping breath.

Ryder knocked on the frail door. All around, dogs started barking and doors slammed. No one around here wanted to talk to any door-to-door fact finders.

Finally, the old slab of wood creaked open with a whine and a grizzly man with a smoky gray beard and missing teeth stared out at them. "What?"

"Brian Purdue?" Ryder asked.

"Who wants to know?"

Ryder flashed his badge. "I do. Are you Brian Purdue?"

The man slammed the door and then they heard fast footsteps heading to the other side of the apartment.

"A runner," Ryder said on a frustrated sigh. "Let's go around."

But Emma wasn't listening. She took off in the other direction from Ryder and hurried around the other side of the fourplex that sat like all the others, side by side like boxes.

She made it around back in time to see Grizzly running as fast as his emaciated body would carry him, his flip-flops echoing a cadence that seemed like a toll of doom.

Ryder sprinted around the other corner and called after the man, "Hey, stop. We just want to ask a few…"

Emma caught up with Grizzly and tackled him around

his scrawny waist and body slammed him to the dirt, her head pounding with each thud. "We need to ask you some questions. So don't be rude, okay?"

"Let me up," the man squealed. "I ain't done nothin'."

"No," Emma said, holding him down. She could smell the fear pouring off him. She couldn't be sure, but he looked like the man who'd been driving that pickup truck. The man who might have taken Reese.

Ryder dropped beside them and said, "I'll take over now."

The look he gave Emma told her not to argue.

"Be my guest."

She sank back on the dirt and grass and took a deep breath, sweat cooling her, dizziness trying to spin around her. She had to be sure. But she prayed this man would tell them the truth and that he could lead them to her missing daughter.

Ryder cuffed Brian Purdue. "Let's take a ride downtown and discuss some outstanding warrants."

"I ain't got nothin' to tell you here nor there," Purdue shouted over his shoulder as Ryder dragged him to the car. "And you," he said, glaring at Emma. "You shoulda stayed out of the Triple B."

"Bingo," Emma said. Then she grabbed Purdue by his dirty T-shirt. "So you did see me there. We have another eyewitness, Ryder."

"I didn't witness nothin'. I'm telling the truth. I won't talk. I don't have any information on nobody."

Ryder remained tight-lipped as he put Purdue in the back of his unmarked car. "Don't try anything, Purdue, or we might just drop you off in a ditch somewhere."

Purdue glared at him, but he didn't move.

Then Ryder looked at Emma. "Get in the car," he said

as he rounded the vehicle. "I'm not done with you either, Emma."

Emma got in but she wasn't sorry. "Good, because I want to talk to Mr. Purdue, too. I think I've seen him somewhere before. Maybe near a coffee shop in the Wood Hills area."

Ryder's eyebrows winged up.

Purdue let out a grunt of frustration.

And Emma prayed they'd both cooperate.

ELEVEN

"What part of let-me-do-the-talking did you miss yesterday?"

Emma sat at the kitchen table back at the ranch and stared up at the man who now stood chastising her. It was late afternoon and a day later, since he'd had a patrol car dump her here last night while he mysteriously managed to stay in the city to work a second shift, trying to get some answers out of Brian Purdue and doing a little surveillance on the Triple B.

Well, she was angry, too. She'd been pacing all day since she couldn't go outside for fear of her life. She felt sure Nancy was tired of Emma's many questions ranging from raising goats to breaking in horses.

Nancy had tried to calm her. "Remember when I told you your emotions could be all over the map? Emma, you've been through a traumatic experience and you're still not steady on your feet. Add to that you shot a man yesterday, and, well, it's natural you're ready to go rogue on us. Let Ryder do some of this legwork while you take it easy."

She hadn't been good at taking that advice. How could she just sit here and do nothing when each second could cost Reese her life?

"What part of I-need-to-be-in-on-this are *you* missing, Ryder?" she asked now. "You forced me to come back here last night while you stayed at the station. I could have helped with the interrogations but instead I spent the night tossing and turning."

"You were exhausted and way too wired," he reminded her with a tired frown. "You've had it tough for days now. I figured you'd be more rested and settled today."

She could say the same about him.

"Well, I'm not," she said instead. "I told you, we're in this together. You said the same thing to me—that we were in this together now. That you'd help me now. Purdue was getting away yesterday, and you're mad that I took him down." Then she shrugged. "Besides, I didn't do a lot of talking. I ran after him."

"But *you* should have let me chase him down and *you* should have stayed out of the way. You're way too edgy and you don't think things through. I can't decide if that's from the head injury or if you're just wired that way."

Grabbing her hair and tugging the roots, Emma asked, "Are you going to do this all night? Because if you are, I'll just go to my room and do some digging on the laptop your mother loaned me."

"No."

"No, we're done? Or no, I can't dig on my own?"

"Yes. I mean, no." He stopped pacing and braced the counter with his hands. "Honestly, I don't even know what I'm trying to say."

Stephanie sauntered into the kitchen, her eyebrows raised in curiosity. "I'm just so happy I'm not the one getting the lecture."

Ryder glared at her and then turned back to Emma. "I guess it's over and done, and we did bring him in for questioning. But he's sealed up like a roll of duct tape."

"You'd told me that," Emma pointed out, feeling a tad contrite since Ryder looked wiped out and he'd just accused her of handling things in a bad way. "Several times."

"I also told you to stay out of my way."

"You're rude," Stephanie said with a teenage scowl. "She just got her memory back and now she wants to take up where she left off. I mean, she's trying to find that girl."

"Yes, that's true," Emma said, giving him her own juvenile scowl. Stephanie didn't know all the details, but she appreciated that the girl was on her side. Because she did want to find Reese, more than anything.

"It's dangerous, memory or no memory," Ryder replied. "And Stephanie, you know I can't discuss cases with you."

"Enough already."

They all looked around to find Nancy standing there with her hands on her hips. "I could hear y'all from the yard."

Kicking off her work boots, she marched into the kitchen in her socks. "Stephanie, start peeling potatoes for dinner. Ryder, go take a shower. And Emma, you can either rest in your room or take a dip in the pool."

"I'll help with dinner," Emma said, embarrassed. "I'm sorry, Nancy. I didn't mean to make a scene."

"Oh, we have several scene stealers around here," Nancy retorted, her gaze moving between her son and daughter.

Ryder bobbed his head. "Which is why I think I'll go to my place for a while. I need some peace and quiet."

With that, he whirled and called out to Spur. The dog came running from his hiding place in the den. Together, they hurried out the back door.

Nancy stared after them. "Ah, quiet at last."

Stephanie burst out laughing. "He is such a drama queen at times."

"Right," her mother said, giving Emma a wan smile.

"Steph, the potatoes are in the pantry and you can peel them in the laundry room sink. Get a bowl for the peelings, please."

Stephanie grabbed a peeling knife without argument, but she made a face all the same.

Emma got up and went to the back window and watched the man and dog and decided they both seemed in a hurry to get out of this kitchen.

"I'm a distraction," she said. "I feel like I'm imposing."

Nancy shook her head. "Stephanie and I like having you here." Then she handed Emma some carrots. "How about you clean and chop these to get your mind centered."

Emma gladly took on the chore, but she kept staring out the window, wondering what was wrong with Ryder. He was angry with her, yes. They'd taken down the man who might know where Reese was, but Ryder wouldn't even let her talk to Brian Purdue.

Because it went against the rules in the same way her taking down Purdue had been against the rules. She knew that better than most, and yes, she could be headstrong and stubborn, but...this time she needed to be tenacious. In spite of all that, she'd thought Ryder would want her in on the interrogation. Instead, she hadn't even been able to watch or listen. But then, Purdue wasn't talking. Maybe Ryder had been wise to keep her on the other side of the wall. She would have gladly strangled the truth out of the man.

Because he knew something. But he was afraid to talk. One afraid to talk, one dead because he talked to Ryder and one dead because he tried to kill her and Ryder the other day.

She still had nightmares about that, but all of these people knew something, and now one of them was sitting in jail in Dallas. What if someone got to Purdue before they could find out the truth?

Emma felt a hand on her arm. Jumping, she found Nancy standing there giving her a sympathetic stare. "You've been holding that carrot for five minutes now. Why don't you go and find Ryder and get this all out of your system?"

"I'm okay," Emma said. "And I'm the last person he wants to see right now anyway." Then she shook her head and lowered her voice. "I feel so helpless. I never got to hold Reese or watch her grow up or any of that. I found her when she was ten, and thankfully the Parkers send me pictures now and then and I check on her on social media, but…when I see you with Ryder and Stephanie I just feel so lost and out of place."

"Is that the same way you felt in all of those foster homes?" Nancy asked while she took over carrot duty.

Emma lifted her chin, realization grabbing at her with a fierce tenacity. "I guess so. I've never thought about it that way, but yes, each time I was moved, I had to start all over again. The last one was hard since I was a teenager and they had two younger children. I wound up being a babysitter, but I loved it. Until I met the boy next door and thought I was in love and…well, you know how that turned out."

Nancy finished the carrots and dropped them in with the bubbling pot roast. "You did what you had to do, Emma. You gave your daughter to parents who love her and want her home. And they called you for help because they trust you. You stayed away out of love, but you came running when they—and your daughter—needed you the most. That takes a lot of courage."

Emma blinked back the tears and turned to Nancy. "But

I failed and here I stand, remembering everything and knowing nothing at all. I don't know what to do next."

"Go for that walk," Nancy said, gently pushing her toward the door. "We've got guards all over the place, so you should be safe. And if you find my ornery son, be gentle with him. He carries the weight of every case on his shoulders."

"Okay." Emma wanted to find Ryder and apologize. She'd been too pushy, too demanding, too reckless. Traits that usually made her good at her job, but those same traits also made her life all the more dangerous.

"Dinner in about an hour," Nancy said. Then she pivoted when Stephanie returned with the peeled potatoes. "Let's get those sliced, and this pot roast will be on its way."

Emma smiled as the two chattered away, amazed at how this family could be arguing one minute and laughing together the next. But then, maybe that's what family was all about. She didn't understand that concept, had never had that kind of bond in her life.

Would Ryder smile when he saw her coming? Or would he tell her to leave him alone and let him do his job?

Spur barked, causing Ryder to look up from the fishing pole he'd been staring at for the last half hour. The fish were too lazy to even bite in this heat, and he really didn't care one way or the other. He thought coming out here in the late-day shade would help him decipher some of the details of this investigation. But all he could do was wonder why he hadn't married and settled down. He could have a good life right here.

But he kept at it, always searching for criminals and lowlifes, that need for justice overtaking anything else that should matter in his life.

When he saw Emma making her way up the old dirt

lane to his cabin by the creek, his heart seemed to care. A lot. He blamed her for bringing out all of these domestic feelings. She'd never had a real home and she'd had to give up the one person she could have loved—her baby daughter.

And that was probably why he'd been so hard on her today. He didn't want to care. He'd held his heart so close over the years, it had grown barnacles. Now those barnacles were peeling away and leaving raw places, all because of a brave woman who was searching for the daughter she'd never known.

Spur took off in her direction, obviously now completely over the female theatrics that had taken place in the kitchen.

Sap.

But Ryder couldn't blame the goofy dog. He felt the same way. Only no one could ever see that. Especially not Emma. She'd put him in his place quicker than an eight-second ride that ended five seconds too soon.

"Hey there," he heard her say to Spur. "You're such a sweet boy."

Ryder gritted his teeth against the cuteness of that. Cute was one thing. Reality was another.

And he dealt with reality every day.

He couldn't handle caring about someone who was as reckless and stubborn as he was. That just didn't factor in his brain.

"Are you catching anything?" she asked, her clean, fresh scent wiping out the mugginess of the day.

"Nope."

"Are you still mad at me?"

"Yep."

"What did I do that was so wrong, Ryder?"

Made me feel again.

He gave up on fishing and pulled the line in and laid the pole on the ground. To the west, the sun was cresting the trees, brilliant and defiant. Just like her. "You put yourself in danger."

"That's not all that's bothering you. You know my job. It's close to what you do. We have to wait and watch and seek and find. Pretty simple."

"But oh, so complicated."

"You're mad because I got in the way? Surely, you're not one of those arrogant thrill seekers who have to always be the hero, right?"

"I'm not a hero. But I don't like… I don't like seeing someone who ignores the rules."

"Like you've never done that?"

She had him there. "That's different. I can take care of myself."

She whirled and stared him down, causing Spur to decide he might want to go off and chase squirrels in the tall pines behind the cabin.

"I can take care of myself, too," she replied, her eyes doing that fire-tipped thing. "I went to a bar because I had a solid lead, and now we have the man in the blue truck in custody."

"I have him in custody, Emma. I have to decide what to do about that since he's not talking, and I really don't have anything except a couple outstanding warrants to keep him there and a judge who'll decide how to deal with him. If his bail is set low, he'll be out of there in a day or so. Right now, he's just a person of interest."

"Yes, a person of interest, and I have proof that he was at that café at the same time as Reese. Maybe something from his truck will give us the truth if the lab can push it through in time." She marched closer and then she tugged at his button-up shirt and looked him in the eye. "I need to talk to him."

"Emma—"

She started beating her fist against Ryder's chest. "In custody, Ryder. And I still don't know if Reese is alive or dead. And you're out here fishing. Fishing." Beat, beat. "And if that means I'm too hotheaded and reckless and that I got in your way, well, I'm sorry, but I want her back and I'll go through you and anyone else who stands between me and finding her." Beat, beat, beat. "Do you understand? Do you?"

Ryder grabbed her fists and stared down into those fiery eyes. "Yes," he said on a whisper. "Yes, Emma, I understand. I do."

She stopped trying to beat him up and collapsed against his chest, her head going limp on his shoulder. "Okay," she gulped. "Okay. I'm sorry…but I just want my baby back. Even if she never sees me or knows I'm her mother, I don't care. I want her back safe and sound and alive. I didn't give her up just to have this awful, unspeakable thing happen to her. Where's the justice in that? If you can't help me, then I'll do it myself. That's how I've always done things. On my own, by myself."

Ryder lifted her chin and wiped at her tears, the agony of her words tearing through him in a way that cut to the core, the softness of her skin soothing against his battered fingers.

He held her head up and looked into her eyes. "You're not alone anymore, Emma. You hear me?"

She nodded, her expression jagged, her eyes raw with pain. And then she laid her head back on his shoulder and finished crying.

Ryder held her there, his calloused heart absorbing her pain like a sponge, taking it all in and accepting it while he prayed they could find her daughter. And alive at that.

TWELVE

They sat on the bank by the water and watched Spur playing in the shallows. Sat silently. Emma had cried herself all out. Now she had that steely determination boiling over inside her again. "We have to get Purdue to talk."

"I know. I left him to stew about the outstanding warrants we found. Petty stuff but he's in trouble enough with the judge to do some time if he can't make bail or give us some answers. I'm sure Pierce will take a turn with him, too."

"You and Pierce, do you usually work all hours of the day and night?"

"Yep."

"That must be tough."

"Probably why we're both bachelors." He stared at the water. "I got close to a woman a couple of years back and she didn't like my way of life—didn't like the danger involved. I missed a couple of dates, we fought and then I saw her with another man. I'm a tad jaded in the love department."

Emma kept her eyes on him and then nodded. "Duly noted. I'm sorry."

"It's okay. We didn't really match anyway."

"I wanted to apologize when I came out here earlier,"

she said, her words low and quiet. "Instead, I had a melt-down."

"You needed a good meltdown. Like I said, you've had a rough time of it lately."

"But that's not me. I've never been a drama queen, and I'm not all touchy-feely."

His bronze-colored eyes moved over her. "Well, that's a shame. Sometimes touchy-feely is just what a person needs."

She pushed at her hair, suddenly shy and nervous around him and aggravated that they couldn't get a break. She'd needed the strength of his arms. It had been a long time since she'd been held that way. But Emma wouldn't allow herself to get used to being in Ryder's arms. They would both move on once…once she knew Reese was safe at home.

So she concentrated on convincing him she could set-tle down. "I know how this works. Going off in a frenzy won't bring Reese home. I have to keep calm and do what I'd do if…if my heart wasn't so into this one."

Ryder gave her a look that made her wish she was still in his arms. "Your heart makes you good at your job, but your head will keep you alive. This has to be the worst kind of torment."

He did understand that part, at least. "It's so hard. I missed out on her life and now—"

"Hey, we're gonna make it, together. We'll get there, but we have to follow procedure or whoever did this could walk free, okay?"

"Okay." Emma took a breath and gazed at the beautiful late afternoon. The sun was settling down for the night, its tones cascading out in pastel hues of pink and golden yellow. "This really is a beautiful spot."

"Glad you noticed."

She almost smiled at that. "Is that your cabin?"

He looked toward where she'd pointed to the right, up on the slope. "Yes. I built it about six years ago."

"You built it?"

"With my bare hands and with wood from old barns and cabins and anything else I could salvage. But I had help."

"It's nice. I'd like to see more of it one day." Emma glanced around and then back to him. "I'm impressed."

Ryder touched a hand to her hair. "I'd love to give you the complete tour sometime."

"You mean, when we're not being shot at or when we're not involved with possible criminals."

"Yeah, maybe then."

The air grew still, but the wind was hot and humid in spite of the shade trees all around them. Ryder kept his eyes on her, a map of emotions spreading through his expression.

"One day maybe we can pick up some burgers—I know all the best burger joints—and come here and have a picnic, and then I'll give you the grand tour. You did say you wanted a good burger."

"I did and you remembered."

"Hard to forget, since you can be kind of demanding." He shrugged at her grimace. "I don't know how to handle you being so quiet and compliant. What do you want me to do next, Emma?"

"Will you let me talk to Purdue?"

"I don't know. Maybe I'll let you sit in. As long as you promise not to knife him."

"I don't carry a knife."

"You do seem calm now."

"My angst is still here…but it's like a festering wound. It just aches all the time."

"I kind of get that," he said. "I still miss my dad, and

I see my mom sitting outside by herself and I know she's been crying. Some wounds can't be healed. My grief has ruined many a relationship. That and my work."

Emma's heart went out to him, but she also took those admissions as a warning. "That pain is what makes you a good detective," she said. "I shouldn't doubt you."

Lowering his head, he said, "Even though I'm sitting here, I have people out there working on this. The whole department is concerned, and you've helped us to fill in some of the puzzle pieces. Plus, now that we've put out more missing person alerts, a lot of volunteers are searching for her, too."

"I want to keep at it. Each moment is precious."

He stood and offered her his hand. "Let's go eat and then we'll hit the files again and compare everything we both know about the Triple B. How's that?"

"I guess it'll keep me busy at least."

"And after supper, if I haven't heard from the people I've got on this, I'll call the station and see what's going on. Any tips or leads, anything I hear, I'll pass on to you."

She let him help her up, and for a moment, he held her, causing her to wonder what it would be like to kiss him.

His gaze moved over her face, his eyes widening in awareness. He leaned in. But his phone buzzed before anything could happen.

With a grunt of frustration, Ryder kept his eyes on Emma and answered. "Palladin."

"I'm on my way," Ryder replied. Ending the call, he turned to Emma. "We've got prowlers on the west side of the property. Two men, armed with high-powered rifles. Get back to the house right now. Spur will go with you. Find Mom and Stephanie and lock the doors. Make sure the alarm is set."

She nodded as he shouted and ran to get his weapon

from the bench where he'd left it by the pond. "I've got to get to the other side of the property."

"How will you do that?" she asked, following him toward his cabin.

"I have a Rhino." He went to a small open garage and showed her the off-road vehicle they used to get around the property. "Go, Emma. Take the path behind the cabin. It's more wooded."

"But Ryder."

"Go now. Spur, take Emma home."

The dog barked and danced and then turned to stare at Emma.

Emma didn't argue. Giving him one last look, she hurried toward the sparse trees that lined the area behind the cabin. Ryder got on the Rhino and took off, but he glanced back once and gave Emma a wave. She hurried toward the woods, Spur barking ahead of her while she prayed Ryder would take care of himself out there.

When she heard shots off in the distant woods, Emma almost turned around. But she'd promised Ryder she'd get to the house and warn his mother and sister. "Let's go, Spur," she said. Then she sprinted toward the house as fast as she could.

"I heard shots," Nancy said when Emma rushed into the house with Spur barking at her heels. "What's going on?"

Emma grabbed at a nearby bar stool to steady herself. Out of breath, she said, "Ryder got a call. Prowlers in the woods."

Nancy took one look at her and put an arm around her waist. "Let's get you to the den. You need to lie down."

"I'm okay," Emma said, her hand on her head, the dizziness not as strong now. "Lock up and set the alarm. And call the hands that are still here and warn them, too."

Stephanie went into motion, scurrying around the house to do as Emma had asked. By the time she'd returned, carrying a rifle and a pistol, Nancy had Emma on the couch with a cold towel over her forehead.

"All clear so far," Stephanie said. "Our men are checking the perimeters of the yard."

"Good," Nancy replied. "Emma, are you still dizzy? Does your head hurt?"

"I'm okay but I'll be better when Ryder comes through the door."

Nancy motioned to Stephanie to sit down. "Stay nearby, honey, until we hear from your brother."

Stephanie sank down on a chair and scrolled through her cell phone apps. But she didn't put up a fight. Ryder had trained his family for just such a scenario.

But Emma had brought a lot of trouble into this house and once she knew he was safe, she intended to remedy that.

She didn't have to wait too long. Thirty minutes later, he came through the door and walked into the den. "I'm all right. We got there too late, but we fired a round to scare them off. Found footprints in the woods and tire tracks up on the road."

"Do you know who it was?" Nancy asked.

"No. Are y'all good?"

"We're fine," Stephanie replied, her eyes wide. "Are you hungry?"

"No."

"Okay, then." Nancy shook her head.

Giving them all a frustrated glance, Ryder turned and left the room.

Emma wondered what Ryder was doing. He'd been holed up in the office for over an hour. Stephanie and

Nancy put away the uneaten food while Emma loaded the dishwasher. No one was very hungry and Nancy stated that the pot roast would hold until later anyway.

"I'll finish up," she said. "You both look tired, but I'm too on edge to sleep."

Nancy and Stephanie gave each other knowing glances and then said their good-nights.

Emma inhaled the quiet and thought about Reese with every breath. Was Reese hungry and afraid, hidden away in some basement or a boarded-up, stifling room? How would they ever find her? Would they find her alive?

Emma had fought to get here and then she'd almost been killed. Now she'd shot a man and people kept coming at her. This had to end. She usually did things her way. Maybe it was time to reinforce that rule.

She thought about the Triple B and what had brought her to Dallas. The man in the blue truck. She'd have to start where she'd left off. Bounce and Ounce were hiding out for some reason. Because she could ID them? Or was someone higher up making them stay hidden because they'd let her live? Those two could have been taken care of since they hadn't done the job.

These people had found her, even here on this vast ranch. Did that mean someone was following them day and night? Ryder had looked so angry earlier, and how could she blame him?

No matter, she had to get back out there. She knew how to lose a tail. Or she used to know how to do that.

The only thing that mattered was her daughter.

Emma finished loading the dishes and stood staring out at the lit-up backyard. A fly couldn't move out there without a light shining on it. Ryder had turned on all the security lights and told his foreman to hire extra men to ride the property.

He should be sleeping, but he wanted to keep everyone safe. Apparently, he'd assigned that job to himself a long time ago. Probably after his father had been murdered. He'd said as much, and he'd declared that he wasn't relationship material.

Some wounds never really heal.

She closed her eyes and prayed for Ryder. Then she prayed for Reese and for the Parkers. Reese's parents were beside themselves with worry, but they had a strong church family to help them through. Her place wasn't with them but out there, finding the girl they all loved.

When a hand touched her arm, Emma opened her eyes and turned to find Ryder standing there. She hadn't even heard him come into the room.

"I would say we'd go for a walk…but…"

He left it at that. She moved past him, the awareness buzzing between them too strong for her tattered nerves to handle. "So now I have to stay inside all the time?"

"Nope. I've been thinking about all of this and I've gone back over every bit of information we'd gathered even before you came into the picture. Like you said, you need to be in the city. I'm going in early tomorrow, and if you want to go with me I'll let you interview Purdue."

Emma ignored the shiver scraping down her spine. He wanted her off the ranch, but she didn't want to be here anyway. These people had her child. She would gladly turn herself over to them if they'd let go of Reese. And it might come to that if they wanted her so much.

"Are you sure, Ryder? Because I need answers and I'm not going to stop until I get them."

Ryder didn't do his usual thing of shutting her down. "I don't see why not. You risked your life to save me and my family. I owe you one."

"I owe you one better," she reminded him. "I'll get the truth out of Purdue."

He held up a warning hand. "I said interview, Emma. Not interrogate."

"I'll work on my charm," she said, her thoughts spinning. "You know, I need a new phone. A burner will do for now. I can make some follow-up calls to the people I've already talked to, in case any of them are trying to reach me."

"We'll take care of it."

"And…can I have my gun back?"

"Not until after you talk to Purdue."

Good point.

"I need to go back to the Triple B."

"Maybe, but only to watch the place. You're not going inside that bar. Bounce and Ounce might be on a little hiatus right now, but anyone who works there will be waiting and watching, whether they want to do so or not. Someone who hangs in the shadows owns that place, and I'm thinking that person is not happy with them or us right now."

She moved from the kitchen to the hallway. "Then maybe we should start there. Dig deep and find out who holds the lease on the Triple B."

"That means digging through records at the courthouse, which can take us down a rabbit hole."

"I can do some online research," she said. "We know the address of the bar, so I'll start there."

Ryder gave her one of his piercing stares, admiration in his gaze. "Do you ever sleep?"

"You're a fine one to talk," she replied as they settled onto a worn creamy leather couch in the small sitting area in the corner of the kitchen. Somewhere in another part of the house, a television blared.

"I know," he said, rubbing his face with his hand. "I

work two shifts a lot of days—and nights. Then I come home and crash. You know how it is. Criminals don't keep normal hours."

"I don't remember dealing with a lot of criminals, but I do know I've sat in parking lots late at night many times, watching cheating husbands or crooked employees."

"Do you like what you do?" he asked, that keen gaze washing over her.

"I thought I did until now," she admitted. "Once I found Reese, I began to see the real reason I'd become an investigator. I really just needed to know she was okay. My worst fear was that she'd be put in the system and that she'd go through some of the things I had to endure. But she was blessed with a good set of parents."

"And now?"

"Now I can see God's hand in the details. What if I'd gone in another direction and never searched for her?"

"Good point. Now you're here and trying to find her. That might not have happened otherwise."

"But why would God lead me here only to have me fail?"

Ryder leaned close and touched a hand to a rebellious strand of her hair. "It ain't over yet. Who says you're gonna fail?"

Emma loved the warmth of his hand as he moved his fingers from her hair to her cheek. "You have a strong faith in spite of being so jaded."

"It's getting stronger by the minute."

"Mine, too. I have to cling to that faith, Ryder. That God brought me here for a purpose. I have to save her."

"I wonder if he brought you here for more, though," Ryder said, his words a husky whisper now.

"And what would that be, Detective?"

"This," he replied.

And then he gave her a slow, gentle kiss that pierced a sweet spot in her soul. Emma gave in to that kiss, a secure feeling cloaking her and covering her.

This couldn't last. It wouldn't last. Too much was at stake for her and her daughter. Kissing a man like Ryder Palladin, who lived for the shadows and worked to fight the worst of mankind, was wrong on so many levels.

But she didn't stop kissing him. Just for these few precious moments, she pretended her world was normal and that everything would be okay. For a few precious moments, Emma melted against Ryder and took in the essence of a man who put his heart and his soul into his work. He'd do that for her, for Reese, because that need to fight for justice was in his blood.

But this couldn't work. Neither of them was the settling-down kind.

Because being with him felt so good but could turn out so bad, Emma pulled away and shot off the sofa and went straight to her room and shut the door, the imprint of his lips still warm on her skin.

THIRTEEN

Ryder didn't sleep very well.

Being across the hallway from Emma seemed to do that to him. Especially since he'd gone and kissed her.

Stupid move, Palladin. And yet, he'd do it again in a heartbeat. Something about kissing Emma had broken all the barriers he'd put up around his tired, jaded heart.

But he had to come up with a new move for now. One that would allow him to do his job and protect Emma, too. He'd have to distance himself from her while still protecting her. He'd help her find the girl, that was a given. But, no matter what, he couldn't get involved with Emma Langston. She obviously wasn't interested in anything permanent anyway, so why was he reading too much into one kiss?

Now he waited for her to come into the kitchen for breakfast, hoping he didn't seem too jumpy. His sister had left for her first day as a church camp counselor for the summer and his mother was out in the barn doing what she loved most, taking care of the animals.

Quiet.

Ryder liked that.

Emma emerged, dressed in her own jeans and a light-weight button-up shirt. And those pointed-toe boots. Even in the heat of summer, like a true Texan, she wore her boots.

"Coffee?" he asked, taking in her messy ponytail and her vivid eyes.

"For the road," she replied, her eyes not quite reaching his. "I'm ready to get going."

So they were going to pretend that kiss hadn't happened? He'd go along with that for now. But sooner or later, they'd have to acknowledge this thing between them. Acknowledge, laugh about it and agree that it could never work.

Or maybe it was all one-sided? On his side.

Ryder found two travel mugs and filled them and then grabbed some toast his mother had left on the counter. "Here, eat this."

Emma took the toast and her coffee and hurried out to his truck, her head down, her steps fast. "I want to get a phone first and then you can drop me off at the courthouse. I'll go to the recorder of deeds office and try to dig something up since I can't get online and find anything. But it'll be tough to find out who owns the Triple B. I mean, they probably have it under a shell account, but I think I can get around that. Or it could be a wild deed—you know—one where no one really knows how many hands it's passed through. Passed through thin air and possibly with just a handshake."

Ryder watched her get into the truck and then he got in and set his cup in the holder while he wondered if she needed any more caffeine. Emma was obviously wired to the hilt. "I know all about wild deeds. Half of this state has probably passed hands that way. It'll be tough, but we do need to find out who owns that bar."

"I can look online, too, if you let me use a computer at the station."

"I'll see what I can do."

"You don't seem so sure, Ryder."

"I said I'll help, but it's gonna be tricky. If this person wants to stay hidden, we both know what that means."

"That we'll be wasting our time." She dropped her napkin and the half-eaten toast onto her lap. "If I have to, I'll go back to the spot where she was taken and start all over again. But Purdue knows something and I aim to find out what it is."

"Okay, we'll talk to Purdue together and then we'll dig through records," Ryder replied. "But first rule—I want you in my sight at all times. No going rogue on me, Emma."

"I just need a phone and a computer," she replied with a daring glare. "And a weapon. I can take things from there."

Ryder followed the on-ramp to the interstate, driving toward Dallas. He'd stop at one of the superstores and get her a burner phone. "I mean it, Emma."

Giving him an indignant glare, she asked, "Are you my keeper?"

"For now, yes." Ryder's frustration turned to anger. "I know you want to find her, but you promised not to go off in a rage, and you seriously need to understand we are dealing with some very dangerous people here."

"All the more reason to keep at it," she retorted. "Just get me to town, Ryder. I won't make trouble, but I'm tired of hiding out on the ranch. It's time to take matters into my own hands."

Ryder decided Emma Langston was the most infuriating woman he'd ever met. "I'm not asking. I'm telling you to be careful. I'm already taking heat for spending so much time with you."

She turned, her ponytail bouncing. "You don't need to do that. Don't neglect your work on my account. I just need some basic things—the phone, maybe some cash that I'll pay back and a place to stay, added to the computer and my gun. So you won't get in trouble at work."

"It's not about work," he said, thinking they'd discuss where to put her later. "I'm losing focus."

"So I'm a distraction. I've told you all along I didn't want to involve your family. Just put me in a safe house and I'll manage."

"You will not manage," he retorted. "Not without me there, too."

Emma's eyebrows winged up like butterflies but her words were husky and low. "I'm trying to help you, Ryder. Trying to give you an out."

"What if I don't want an out, Emma?"

"Then I'm trying to give myself an out."

Ryder gave her a quick scowl and then kept his eyes on the road until they were at the station. No point in arguing with the woman. But he would make sure she never went anywhere alone, even if he wasn't the one with her. And he wouldn't forget that kiss that had seared him to his toes. Or the way she'd just looked at him when she'd told him she was trying to get away from him. Giving him an out? Maybe the kiss was bothering her, too.

"I'm glad you decided to come to work today," Pierce quipped when Ryder dropped down into his squeaky desk chair and let out a grunt. Glancing to where Emma had settled at an old unused desk with a new, go-fast laptop and a still-in-the-box phone, he added, "And I see you brought your new partner with you."

"Jealousy does not become you," Ryder said. "Look, I'm exhausted and just a tad irritated from being shot at on my own property, so if you've got a beef with me,

Daughtry, well, get in line. That woman is not too happy with me either."

"Ah, your first quarrel. So sorry that this relationship has gone sour so soon. But that's par for the course with you, huh?"

"Yep, one of many quarrels," Ryder said on a low note. He didn't add that this one was different. She didn't care about what he did for a living because she came close to doing the same thing. "She's as hard-nosed as me, I think. So I wouldn't exactly call this a relationship."

"Maybe you've finally met your match, cowboy."

"Could be. She wants a go at Purdue."

"Purdue isn't going to talk," Pierce said. "I've had a round or two with him. He refuses to give up anything and he's lawyered up already."

"Oh, yeah?" Ryder sat up straight. "Who's his lawyer?"

"John Clayton."

Ryder let out a whistle. "*The* John Clayton."

"The one and only," Pierce replied.

"He's pretty high up," Ryder said. "Only works for wealthy clients."

"Tell me," Pierce retorted. "He says unless we have a good reason to hold his client, Purdue walks. Doesn't matter about the outstanding warrants. They can be taken care of since they're petty."

"And since someone knows the judge?"

"Maybe." Pierce shrugged. "Clayton says he'll be back with bail money and he'll have the outstanding warrants dismissed so we can't hold Purdue on that."

Ryder couldn't believe this. Who had that much power and why were they willing to risk taking a chance on a lowlife like Purdue?

Before he could form an idea, Emma came up to his

desk. "I'm ready to go to the courthouse. I talked to one of the clerks and she's already on the search."

"Search for what?" Pierce asked, skeptical.

"Records," Emma replied, her tone sure and steady. "I'm going to find out who owns the Triple B. Whoever it is, they have to be hiding something. I'm tired of running for my life. I have to find Reese Parker before it's too late."

She shot Ryder a pointed stare. "I'll be waiting in the lobby." Then she turned and hurried around the corner.

Pierce shook his head after she marched away. "I get what you mean," he told Ryder. "Bossy, ain't she?"

"Demanding and desperate," Ryder replied, standing and walking backward while he talked to Pierce. "She wants to find her daughter."

Pierce nodded, his expression softening. "Well, she does have a point about digging into the Triple B more. Meantime, what can I do to help?"

Ryder decided he could use all the help he could find, and since he had something niggling at his gut, he said, "Why don't you call the station that reported about Emma's assault and find out who tipped them off? And you might call in some favors regarding John Clayton's clients. A list would sure help."

"On it," Pierce said. "What makes you think the news people were tipped off? You know they have scanners, right?"

"Yes, but don't you find it odd that only one station out of the half-dozen main stations reported on this? Add that to how the sheriff's substation out at Wood Hills dragged their feet on the missing girl and I'd say someone is paying off a lot of people."

"Are you sure?"

"I haven't verified but…I think we should look into that angle and talk to the reporter who leaked the incident."

"Which translates, 'Hey, Pierce, can you look into this for me?'"

Ryder was now almost to the lobby. "Didn't I just say that?"

"Yeah, I reckon you did." Pierce stood and shook out the kinks. "You go after Boss Lady while I find out about the news report."

"I'll check back with you later," Ryder said.

"Oh, I'm still waiting to hear on Dumpster prints," Pierce said. "We're stalled for now."

"Not if I can help it," Ryder replied. He hurried around the corner, thinking Emma had managed to slip right past him to go to the lobby. What if she'd kept on going?

She could keep walking. Just head right on out the door and call a cab now that she had some cash. Her ID was in her wallet and she had one credit card that she hoped wasn't maxed out. Emma had worked with less.

She eyed the door and then checked behind her. Ryder must still be talking to his partner. Emma inched closer. The door was right there and the desk sergeant was on the phone.

"Hey!"

She whirled and saw Ryder stalking toward her, a dark scowl thundering across his face. Why did the man have to look so good, even when he was in a mood? His dark hair swirled around his tan skin and his eyes held a dare that only made her want to run toward him, not away from him.

Her one chance was over.

"Going somewhere, Langston?"

"I'm standing right here, Palladin."

He caught up to her. "Yeah, right. I told you to stay in sight."

"And I told you, you are not my keeper."

"Don't be difficult. We're both on the same team."

Emma's shame must have shown on her face because his scowl went soft. "You're right," she said. "I don't know why I'm taking this out on you. I guess because I feel so helpless. And when I feel that way, I kind of get impulsive and go off on any tangent. I know you're doing all you can to help."

Ryder held her arm as they walked out, his alert eyes scanning the parking lot and surrounding buildings. "Did I just hear an apology? Was that in there somewhere?"

"Okay, I'm sorry. Sorry that I ever got you involved and very sorry that I have to depend on you to help me."

"Again, not feeling sincerity in your apology."

She stopped at his truck. "I'm sorry, Ryder. I'll try to follow procedure from now on. I… I have to keep moving, doing, or I'm going to go crazy."

"I understand," he said, his eyes holding her there in the hot sunshine. "But we need to work together. I can't get my work done if I'm worried about your running out on me, Emma."

"Has someone done that to you, before?" she blurted and then instantly wished she could take it back. From the haunted look on his face, apparently she'd guessed correctly.

"Nobody that mattered," he said. "Now let's go."

FOURTEEN

Hmm.

Emma took in that comment and wondered who had hurt this man. Or maybe he'd been the one to do the hurting? She didn't want to know and she didn't want to ask. Okay, she did want to know, but she couldn't ask. Not right now. She had other things on her mind. Like that kiss they'd shared. The kiss she was trying so hard to forget.

They made it to the courthouse, and Emma got out and rounded the truck to meet him. "We'll be working with Mrs. Mildred Cross. And from her attitude, she lives up to that name."

Ryder grinned. "I've worked with her before. Tough as shoe leather. But good at tracking down information."

When they got inside and saw Mrs. Cross hobbling toward them, Emma had to hide her surprise. The woman wasn't much over four feet tall, but her orthopedic shoes gave her a bit more height. Staring at them through thick red glasses, she touched a hand to the floral scarf tied around her throat and somehow managed to look down on them even though she was looking up at them.

"So you called earlier?"

"Yes," Emma said, trying not to be intimidated. "About

the Triple B." She named the location of the bar. "Were you able to find out anything?"

Mrs. Cross turned her shrewd gaze to Ryder. "I do believe you've been in before."

"Yes, ma'am," he said, leaning in with a lazy grin. "And you sure were helpful. I told my friend here you were the best person for this job. We're looking for a missing teenaged girl, and while we can't discuss the details, we believe the Triple B is owned by someone high up, know what I mean?"

"So you're implying that this disreputable bar could be owned by someone who is hiding behind a stellar reputation?" She waited a stern beat and added, "And that this bar is somehow connected to the missing girl?"

"Yes, ma'am. We're afraid so, but we need some proof, something to go on. Can you help us?"

"A child is missing. It's my civic duty to help, don't you think?"

"I would sure hope so," Ryder replied.

Surprised that the woman had asked about the circumstances of the case and that Ryder had offered up information, Emma watched in amazement while Mildred's disapproving scowl turned into an appreciative smile. "I'd be glad to. I don't like it when people push themselves off as something they are not, and I surely don't want any harm to come to a young girl."

Emma bit her lip to keep from crying, and she really wanted to hug Mrs. Cross right now but knew that might be a big mistake on her part. She wanted to hug Ryder even more. He'd deliberately dropped enough hints to win over the woman's support. Remembering his kiss, Emma decided she'd settle for getting to those records.

Giving Emma a steady stare, Mrs. Cross said, "It would

help if you had a name, but we can work around that for now. Let's do some digging."

Two hours later, they'd discovered a lot of things about the Triple B, but they didn't have a lead on who now owned the place.

"Definitely a handshake kind of deal," Mrs. Cross said on a final note of defeat. "But…I have ways of finding out things." Glancing at the clock, she added, "We'll be closing soon, so why don't you two go on about your business and I'll start fresh tomorrow."

"You're a trouper, Mrs. Cross," Ryder said, fatigue lining his features.

"Call me Mildred," she replied with her own tired smile. Then she turned to Emma. "I hope you find the young girl."

"Thank you," Emma said, steeling herself against that knife-edged pain.

They left, feeling the strain of the day. Emma didn't normally get this tired, but she had to remind herself that she'd suffered a head injury just a few days ago. Would she ever feel herself again?

Looking over at Ryder once they were back in his truck, she wondered if she should have her head *reexamined*. The man did things to her system that left her dazed and confused.

"You're a real charmer," she said to counteract those erratic feelings swirling like tumbleweeds inside her head. "Mildred is smitten."

"Mildred is married and has eight grandchildren," he replied. "Or else, I'd snatch her up in a New York minute."

Emma actually laughed at that. But the laughter died on her lips. "So we know that the Triple B had passed hands several times and that the building has reinvented itself.

Restaurants, retail clothing, once an insurance company and now a bar."

Ryder nodded, his eyes on the heavy afternoon traffic out of town. "And we have a list of previous owners but not the current one. We'll research those names more tonight."

"I need to find a hotel or apartment to stay in temporarily," she said. "I have some addresses."

"And I have a better idea."

Emma twisted on the seat. "I can't go back to the ranch, Ryder. We discussed this."

"What if you went back but no one knew you were there, not even my workers?"

"How would I do that? Just drive up and run into the house?"

"No. The cabin."

Her heartbeat shot up and caught in her throat. "Your cabin? Are you serious?"

"Yes. We sneak you in after dark. I go back and forth as if I'm there alone like I've done for years. All will seem normal. I'll put out the word that you're staying in town."

"And you think that word will drift through the air to the people holding Reese?" She shook her head. "No, I can't go back to the ranch. Period."

"Emma, if someone on the ranch is passing information, I need to know."

"You think you have a mole working for you?"

"I don't know. But I don't like how we had intruders on the ranch so soon after the first one."

Emma cringed, remembering she'd killed a man. "Another reminder of why I should find somewhere else to hide out."

He pulled the truck into a shopping center and turned off the engine. "Emma, it's too dangerous."

"I know that. I'll be careful. But it's taking up time,

going back and forth to the ranch when I could be pounding the pavement and asking questions."

"That didn't go very well before."

"Then let me do surveillance with you as we planned. If you insist on me staying at the ranch, then I'll be up and ready to go to work with you each day. I'll find a quiet corner and I won't pester anyone. If I go out, you can send someone with me."

He studied her for a moment. "Okay, let's compromise. We have a safe house here in town. It's not much and sometimes if I'm working double shifts I sleep over there if it's not in use. If we have late nights, we can stay there. Or you can stay there and I'll put a guard on you. In between we head out to the ranch, just to throw anyone off."

Emma listened and thought about what that could mean. Maybe if she got things accomplished and found a good lead, she could leave the safe house and get on with her mission here. Even if she had to take someone with her. Even if she had to take Ryder with her. What choice did she have? She could force the issue and just go out on her own, but they both had reasons to work together on this. She needed the resources he could provide and he needed her to help with the Triple B takedown.

But agreeing to this would mean they'd be together almost 24/7. How could she balance her need to find her daughter with the confusing feelings she had for this man?

"All right, we'll start there," she finally said. "I'm going to work day and night to find Reese."

"Understood."

He cranked the truck and turned it toward the frontage road that would get them to the interstate.

Emma stared into the afternoon sun.

Then she heard a boom, and the windshield of the truck

shattered. Ryder stopped the truck and went into action, pushing her head down as another shot rang out.

"They've found us again," he said, his breath warm on her skin.

Ryder held her down and waited. "I've got to get us off the road and away from other cars," he said. "Stay down, Emma."

He lifted up and shifted into Reverse, then took off toward the large shopping center parking lot again. Finding a space away from the busy area close to the strip mall, he pulled up underneath a towering oak and cut the motor.

"Are we safe yet?" Emma asked, her head still down, her hair falling over her head and shoulders like a blanket.

"I don't see anyone else pulling into the parking lot," he said. Then he noticed an embankment near the spot where they'd been shot at.

Ryder squinted into the traffic and trees. "They must have been waiting for us to leave the courthouse. Then they probably drove right past us on the road when we stopped earlier. They had to pull over and wait up on that embankment."

Emma lifted her head and eyed the bank of grass and trees. "Or they knew our route and staked out a sniper hole."

"I love it when you talk logistics," Ryder said on grim tone. "But yeah, somebody is watching our every move. They probably planned to shoot out a tire on the interstate, but when I pulled off they waited and then took a shot."

He lifted her up and stared over at her. Ryder admired the way she summed things up, but then she'd been on the police force before she became a PI. Maybe that was why he was so attracted to her. She spoke his language. And that was probably why he was fighting the attraction.

They'd butt heads on everything and make each other miserable. This kind of life did not hold out hope for domestic bliss, after all. So he pushed aside the memories of his mother crumbling to the floor when two sheriff's deputies had come to the ranch to tell her that her husband had been shot and killed. He never wanted to put a woman through that kind of pain.

"I don't know how to keep you safe."

"Then stop trying. Let's draw them out."

"Okay, I don't love it when you talk like that."

"Look, every minute is precious," she said, her eyes full of apprehension. "They want to shut me down, and that makes me believe they have Reese. She's still alive."

"For now."

"So we have to stay at it. They can keep coming all they want, but I need to be away from the ranch. It's too dangerous for your family, Ryder."

"I'm not so sure the safe house will work either," he said. "For tonight we can go there and later we'll sneak back to the ranch and you can stay in the cabin. I'll sleep on the couch."

Emma's expression changed on that. "Is that a good idea?"

"It's my cabin." Then he said, "I have two bedrooms but…the couch has a better vantage point of the yard, okay?"

"Okay."

Glad that was settled, Ryder watched the parking lot for a few more minutes. Then he got out and edged around the truck to see the damage, all the while aware that the shooter could be lying in wait.

Soon, he was back at the wheel. "Just shot up the windshield, obviously aiming for one of us," he said. "I'm taking us to the station so I can have our techs go over the truck.

They might find a bullet or two. We'll take an unmarked loaner home. That might throw them off."

"I'm not closer to finding Reese than I was before," Emma said. "Once we're home, I'm going to call that list of her friends again and go back over her social media habits."

Ryder didn't know what to tell her. But he wanted to make her see she wasn't alone in this. "You know I've got people searching and pounding the pavement. Her photo has been posted on every local news channel, and volunteer organizations are passing around her photo and sharing it on social media. Her parents are working hard on this, too. That's a broad network, Emma."

"I know," she said, "but I'm going nuts just thinking about her. Is she cold, hungry, scared? All of those things, I'd think. Is she wondering if she's been forgotten, abandoned, the way I abandoned her?"

"Hey, you didn't abandon her. You did what you thought best for your baby."

"If I'd kept her, we might not be here now."

"But you can't predict what might have happened back then or now," Ryder said. "You're here now to help her, so that has to count for something."

"Not if I don't find her."

Ryder got an idea. He turned off the service road and headed to the station. "Let me get us a vehicle," he said, not planning on telling Emma his plan too soon. "You can wait in the reception area, where plenty of patrolmen are roaming around."

"I'll do that since I'm starting to wonder if someone on the inside either there or at the ranch *is* a snitch for whoever is after us."

Ryder left that comment alone for now, but he had to

agree with her. Things didn't add up. Who was watching them…and could that person be someone close to him here on the force or at home?

FIFTEEN

They made it back to the station without any more incidents, but Emma's discomfort only continued to grow. She watched everyone who walked by, wondering if there was a dirty cop among the people Ryder worked with and trusted. Now she didn't feel safe here or out at the ranch. Somehow, she had to find a way to do this on her own, no matter the danger.

Pierce looked up from his desk and gave her a nod. He seemed to resent her presence here. Could he be the one who sent people to shoot her?

She couldn't believe that since he and Ryder worked so smoothly together in spite of their sarcastic banter, but she had to be careful anyway. Since she'd lost all of her contacts along with her phone, she called Reese's mother and asked her to text all the numbers of Reese's close friends. Emma planned to call the five or six girls and couple of boys who knew Reese and hung out with her on a regular basis. Maybe one of them would remember something since she was pretty sure she'd done that already. But jarring them all again couldn't hurt. She prayed that these bad people hadn't called any of her contacts to harass or threaten them, but she had no way of knowing.

Her new phone buzzed a few minutes after she'd talked

to Annette Parker. "Annette?" she asked, wondering if Reese's mother had forgotten someone's name and number.

"Emma, I remembered something," Annette said, her voice trembling. "One of Reese's friends called here a few days after she disappeared. She seemed rattled and upset, but then we all were. I tried to feel her out, but she acted so strange and then she said she had to go. I made a note to call her back the next day. We left to place fliers about Reese around the neighborhood, and we got home rather late and went to bed. Then we heard about you the next morning and, of course, we were worried for your safety, as well. I found the note underneath some mail on my desk right after we talked earlier. I should have mentioned this to you sooner."

"That's okay," Emma said, thinking of the tremendous stress the Parkers were under. "Give me the name and I'll call her right now."

"Tessa Clark," Annette replied. She gave Emma the number. "She was with Reese that day, but Tessa is very shy. She rarely came to our home, but Reese felt sorry for her and tried to bring her out of her shell by including her in things. Tessa made the effort to call me, so it had to be important. I can't believe I forgot to alert you."

"It's all right, Annette," Emma said. "I'll take care of it. I'll let you know if I hear anything new."

Emma ended the call, the anguish in Annette's voice mirroring the anguish in her soul. When would this end?

She glanced up and saw Ryder coming toward her. "Hi," she said when he sat down next to her.

"Hey," he replied, his gaze heated as always. "I have some information."

Emma's heart pumped with fear and dread. "What?"

"Remember I told you that we scraped DNA from underneath your fingernails and also gathered some hair and clothing fibers off Junior?"

"Did you get a match?"

He nodded. "Ounce, better known as Eddie Culpepper. And some traces that match Bounce, better known as Sam Pittman."

"So that proves they attacked me and left me for dead and that they killed Junior—or at least were with him the night he died."

"Yes, and then they both went to ground. No sight of them in the great state of Texas. But we'll keep looking. That kind of scum can't stay hidden forever." Then he scratched his head. "And Petey Smith, the man you shot, had a long list of crimes to his name. He probably hired on through someone else who offered him money. We need to find out who that someone was."

Emma shook her head. "I'll never get over killing him but…he was coming for you."

"You made the right call," Ryder said. "Hey, I'm not complaining."

Emma let it go. "So we keep staking out the Triple B and hope one of them pops up," she said, relief mixed with regret in her mind. "We haven't been able to pin down anyone we've seen so far in the surveillance videos or photos. Other than seeing Brian Purdue's truck parked there, we don't have much to go on regarding who's behind all of this."

Ryder grunted. "So we can place Bounce and Ounce at two scenes connected to this investigation, and we can place Brian Purdue at the Triple B and at the site where Reese was taken. You tracked him there and…we tracked him down."

"But he's not talking," Emma finished. "And you'll have to let him go if that lawyer shows up."

"Yep. But the fancy lawyer has kind of stalled out on that thread." He glanced around, a frown twisting his face.

"Hey, what are you thinking?" Emma asked, wondering where his mind had gone. His expression was etched in fatigue and sadness.

"Oh, just stuff," he said. "Back to the Triple B. We've been doing rotations on watching the place, but yeah, I'd like to personally keep an eye out over there. And you can go with me as long as you promise not to go all cowgirl on me. Understood?"

Bobbing her head, she said, "Understood."

"I have a possible lead, too." She explained about Tessa Clark. "I'm going to call her right away."

"Okay." Ryder gave her a long, determined stare. "I'll tell Pierce he and the others can take a break tonight. You and I will stake out the Triple B for the next few nights and then Pierce can take over during the day. Now that we have solid evidence that places Bounce and Ounce at the scene when you were attacked and as possibly being Junior's murderers, we can go after them and hit hard. If we ever find them, that is."

"Who's running the place while they're away?" she asked, thinking maybe he'd let her go in and find out.

"They keep rotating people—all kinds of unsavory people move through there. Hard to keep up." Then he scratched at his five o'clock shadow. "But maybe if I go in and push—"

"I'll go with you."

"You'll wait in the car."

"I can disguise myself. I've done that before."

"Too risky, Emma. You are high on their radar and I have to be careful, too, since some of them could have seen us the night we found you."

"Fine. Let's get going. I'll call Tessa on the way."

She followed him to the unmarked navy sedan a patrolman had pulled up close to the building. Once inside, Emma waited until he was out in traffic and then punched in the number Annette Parker had given her.

"Hello."

The voice sounded feeble and distressed.

"Tessa Clark?"

"Yes."

"This is Emma Langston. Annette Parker gave me your number. I'd like to talk to you about Reese Parker. Do you know something that can help us locate her?"

"No. I shouldn't have called Mrs. Parker. Never mind."

The girl hung up.

Emma stared at the phone and called back. The girl didn't pick up, so she left a message. "If you change your mind, call this number. Please, Tessa. It's important."

"Not a good sign," Ryder said after she'd ended the message. "If that girl knows something but she's running scared, that could mean someone has threatened her, too."

Emma nodded. "And that also means we need to find her before they do something worse than threaten her."

"First thing tomorrow, we track her down."

Emma knew he was right. Since it was getting late and they really needed to check out the Triple B, she couldn't force him to drive to Tessa's house. "Okay. First thing tomorrow. Meantime, I'll keep calling her."

Ryder pulled the car up to the curb a few yards away from the rickety front door of the Triple B. "We've had people on this place since your attack but nothing we can use so far. But you never know what might happen."

Emma let her window down to get a breeze, the scent of barbecue and burgers making her stomach growl. "Not that I want to eat in there, but I am so hungry."

"We'll eat later," he said. "I should have stopped for some fast food."

"I'm too nervous anyway," she admitted. "I used to be cool and calm. I need to find my game face again."

"I like the face you're wearing."

"Ha." Taking a breath, she held up her damp hair. "So what did you and Pierce have so far on the Triple B?"

"Obviously not much," he replied. "It's been a long, hot summer. We kept hearing of smuggling going on here. An informant told us they move drugs and guns through here on a regular basis. Then we heard they might be running an escort service."

Emma started fidgeting. "Did you find any proof of that?"

"We were getting close when you showed up," he said, his eyes on the door of the seedy bar. "We had a warrant for one of the locals who hung out here—our man Petey as a matter of fact. A gofer. Did the kind of odd jobs most people don't have the stomach for. But he got away the night Pierce found you in the alley. Ran out the back door, and Pierce came around the building but Petey was gone. Who we now know to be Bounce and Ounce saw Pierce and took off back into the bar and locked the back door. Pierce saw you lying there and radioed me."

"While they escaped out the front door."

"Most certainly."

"What if they're both dead, too?"

"That's a possibility. If they were supposed to take care of you and they failed, they might have both been permanently demoted."

Emma stared at the building, memories cloaking her with the same misty heaviness of the awful summer humidity. "I walked right in there and started asking around.

I knew better but I was so scared and desperate. I couldn't bear to think of Reese locked away in there."

"Did you try to search for her?"

"No. I couldn't get past all the guards." She stopped, her mind whirling. "They guard both doors and there's a staircase down past the bar. Maybe a basement." She pushed at her hair. "I remember people coming and going. Bounce came up from those stairs and escorted me out the back door."

"So we don't know what's down there."

"I can only guess. Reese could be hidden down there in the dark and heat." Her fingers worked at the door handle, the panic setting in. Her breathing became shallow and a cold sweat popped out like blisters along her spine. "I... I can't sit here, Ryder. I have to see for myself."

He grabbed her other hand. "Emma, no. You can't rush in there and demand to see her. They'll kill both of you."

"Then you go," she said, her breath caught in her throat. "Go in there and do your job."

Ryder turned to her and took her, his hands gripping her arms. "Take deep breaths. You're having a panic attack."

"No, I'm angry. I want my daughter. I can't do this anymore, Ryder."

The panic filled her, consuming her. She couldn't breathe, couldn't move. She grabbed hold of Ryder, the thick, hot air around them pulling her down.

"Emma, look at me," he said, his gaze meeting hers. "Emma."

She gulped in air, tears streaming down her face. "Let me go."

"Not until you're calm. You can't go in there. Not like this." He placed his hand on her cheek. "I won't let them hurt you again."

Emma crumbled under the tenderness of his words, his eyes, his hands holding her steady.

Ryder pulled her close, tugging her head against his chest. "I'll go in and ask around. If I'm not back in thirty minutes, you take this car and leave, understand?"

She bobbed her head. But she knew in her heart she wouldn't leave him in there. She'd go in after him.

"Will you be all right?" he asked.

"I'm better. I… I used to have panic attacks growing up in the foster system, but I thought I was over them."

"You've been through a lot. It's understandable. But I won't leave you if you're still shaky."

"I'm fine," she said on a snap while she straightened her spine. "Now go."

But before Ryder could get himself together enough to leave the car, he lifted away from her. "Emma, we've got movement."

She looked past him and saw two men and a young woman exiting the building. The men wore jeans and button-up shirts and the girl had short blond hair and wore a knee-length sleeveless dress and flip-flops. To anyone passing by, it looked as if friends were leaving the bar together.

But Emma sensed something else. The girl looked around, fear streaming off her expression. She looked way too young to be in such a place.

Emma let out a breath. "It's not her. It's not Reese."

"No, but we can't get a good look."

Emma started snapping photos with her phone. "Maybe the techs can clean these up."

"Let's hope."

"Ryder—"

"I know," he said. "We'll follow them."

Emma couldn't argue with that. "That's not Bounce and

Ounce and that's not Reese," she said. "But I'd sure like to know where they're going."

Ryder let the car idle while he waited to see what the trio would do. They rounded the building.

"There's a run-down parking lot on that side of the bar," he said, waiting. "Let's see if they drive out."

"What if they're walking?"

"I can't get any closer. They might make us."

They waited and Emma held her breath and tried to recover from her panic attack and from the way Ryder had held her. He made her feel safe and warm and…secure.

She'd never had any real security of her own. Maybe that was why she worked so hard to help others feel more secure and settled. But…could she trust her own heart with these newfound feelings? She'd never opened her heart to anyone. But now her heart betrayed her each time she was with this man who lived in the shadows and ran on adrenaline and danger. That scared her more than the bad memories that kept popping into her head.

Pushing the roar of emotions away, she watched the building. Another man emerged from the bar. "Ryder?"

Ryder squinted into the darkness. "That's John Clayton. He's the big-shot lawyer who came to visit Brian Purdue. Has the kind of clientele that can pay big bucks to make things go away."

"Or people?" Emma asked, the tension inside her soul building with each word. "Can he make people go away?"

Ryder shot her a grim nod. "Especially people."

SIXTEEN

"Should we follow *him* or the others?" Emma asked, her voice still low and husky. "Or maybe we *should* go inside and ask around."

"Let's see." Ryder waited for the lawyer to get in his fancy black sedan. "They might all be going to the same place."

Emma hit a hand on the dash. "How do we decide? I want to storm that place and search every cockroach corner, but my gut is telling me to follow what's in front of us."

"I agree," he said, again admiring how her brain worked. "Let's see which way they go."

After what seemed hours but was only minutes, two cars finally exited the back parking lot.

"Here we go," Ryder said, holding the car in place. "Let's let them get going so they won't see us."

Emma fidgeted with her seat belt and then held her phone up again to snap pictures of the vehicles. "Maybe we can zoom in on the license plates. Hurry, Ryder."

The two cars both went east, away from downtown. Ryder counted a few beats and hit the gas to follow them. "Interesting. They must have had a meeting. I wonder who the girl is."

"I don't know," Emma said. "Whoever she is, she's scared."

Ryder could see that same fear in Emma's eyes. "It wasn't Reese," he reminded her.

Emma shook her head. "I wish it had been her. I could have at least approached them and pulled her away."

"We're following them," he reminded her. "We might be able to help this girl."

"I hope so. And I hope they lead us to wherever they have Reese hidden."

The unspoken things between them tore at Ryder's heart. Reese Parker could be alive, and he prayed they'd find her alive. But they had to accept that the worst could happen, too. That hung between them in a heavy fog. Emma would be devastated and he'd feel the guilt of not saving her daughter. Could he live with that? Could they move on together after that?

He doubted it. So he pushed away the image of holding Emma in his arms and concentrated on the cars ahead of them on the frontage road that ran beside the busy main highway.

"They're not getting on the freeway," she said.

"Nope. Probably taking a back way to wherever they're headed."

Ryder's cell buzzed but he kept his eyes on the vehicles making their way out of the city. "Palladin."

"Hey, man, I've got some information that kind of changes everything," Pierce said.

"I'll take it."

"We got word back about that media leak regarding Emma's attack."

Ryder glanced over at Emma. Her eyes held a questioning look. "Tell me."

"Bobby Doug Manchester apparently leaked the attack to the press."

"I figured as much," Ryder said, his gaze on the cars turning left ahead of them. "He's been talking to the chief about crime in that area. Just turning the screws like he always does."

"I have more," Pierce said. "We went over all the photos and snapshots we've managed to get on the Triple B, even cleaned up some of the video."

"And?"

"We have two grainy photos and a still shot from our own surveillance video showing the night Emma was attacked. I think one of the men in those pictures and video is Bobby Doug."

Ryder let that soak in, his mind boiling over with speculation. "You're saying he could have been there that night?"

"I'm saying someone who looks a lot like him could have been there. We have a lot of unidentified prints from the Dumpster. We ran some of the best ones back through the system, and guess who matched?"

"Are you kidding?"

"No, man. Bobby Doug was in the military for eight years. His prints are on file. I ran 'em after I saw the photos."

"They're a match?"

"They're a match."

"His lawyers will tear this apart in about five minutes, but if we can find more evidence we might have a case."

"I think so," Pierce said. "Do you want me to run this by Brian Purdue? I mean he's just sitting here and this could scare him into talking."

"Or scare him into clamming up," Ryder replied.

"We can't hold him much longer," Pierce reminded him.

"I know but hold off," Ryder said. "We're tailing some

folks who came out of the Triple B. I'll call you later and hopefully we can put it all together then."

Pierce ended the call and Ryder turned to Emma. "I think we finally have a credible case, Emma."

Emma kept watching the vehicles ahead of them. "Ryder, the lawyer's turning left."

Ryder looked at the blinkers on both cars. "And the other car is going right."

"Which one do we follow?"

Ryder glanced over at her. "The girl?"

"The girl," she said, relief coloring her words. "But we can put a tail on the lawyer, too, right?"

"I was thinking that, yes."

"Once we see where they're headed and decide what we can do, then you can tell me about that phone conversation."

"I will," he said, hitting Pierce's name on his phone. He told Pierce what had happened and gave him the location, a description of the vehicle and the name of the road where John Clayton had turned off.

Then he checked on Emma. She gave him a quick nod and then focused on the vehicle they were following. Maybe he and Emma could have a future together after all. She sure knew how his mind operated.

Emma wanted to know what Ryder had found out but she was so afraid they'd lose the car up ahead she didn't want to distract him. Her heart beat against her chest each time the car accelerated or took a turn.

"They seem to be going in circles."

Ryder did his grunt thing. "They might have figured out that someone is following them."

He pushed the car closer so they could merge in with the few cars on the road. Then he checked the rearview mirror.

"Emma, we got trouble."

"What?" She glanced into the passenger-side mirror and saw a big pickup truck barreling toward them. "Now we're being followed?"

"Looks that way," Ryder said, shifting into the other lane.

Now they were right behind the car they'd been tailing for twenty minutes. Emma took another picture of the plates.

"How do they always find us?"

"Because they have someone watching us same as we're watching them."

"So what do we do?"

"We try to beat them at their own game," Ryder said, speeding up.

"Ryder, the car ahead will spot us for sure if you get tight on their bumper."

"I hope so," he said. "We'll all get together that way."

He immediately radioed for backup. Then he turned to Emma. "Send Pierce a copy of that last photo. He can run the plates."

Emma did as he asked and then said, "If you force the issue, will that help us?"

"It might," he said. "If I do it the right way."

Emma didn't want to take his mind off his driving, but her first concern was Reese. If they pushed back too much, something might happen to her daughter. "I don't like this."

"Neither do I, but hey, they started it."

Ryder pushed the vehicle up close to the one they were following, his intent obvious. He wanted to provoke them. But she wasn't sure why.

Ryder eased forward, tapping the car that seemed intent on getting away. But the car behind them was about to do the same thing to them.

"What's the plan, Palladin?" she asked, willing to go along.

"Hold on. That's your plan. Just hold on and trust me."

Emma didn't think now would be a good time to tell the man she had major trust issues. "Okay."

He maneuvered the car closer to the sedan caught in traffic and bumped at the sleek car, a bit harder this time.

"Are you ready?" he asked. "Holding tight?"

"I'm holding my breath," she replied.

He waited and watched as the car behind them started coming too fast. And then, at the perfect moment for impact, he swerved to the left lane and took off as fast as he could.

The two cars behind them collided with a bang and went into a spin that left them both twisting in the hot wind.

Emma braced while the sound of the crash hit the hot night air. "A pileup, involving two cars."

"Exactly. And patrol cars in route."

He stopped the vehicle at a gas station and hurried to get out. Emma followed suit. They watched as the two cars tried to come apart, bumpers and headlights crunching and crushing against each other. One car had crashed into a tree and the other one had crashed into it. Twice, if she'd counted correctly.

Then Emma gasped. "Look."

Ryder stared into the night, his cell phone recording all of it. "The girl's running away."

"Let's go after her."

They got back into the car and started back toward the side street where they'd last seen the girl.

But by the time they managed to get around the accident and onto that street, the young girl was nowhere in sight.

* * *

An hour later, they still hadn't found the girl. She'd taken off through a strip mall lined with restaurants and boutiques. Ryder figured she'd either ducked into a restaurant to call for help or she'd gone into a shop and bought different clothes and a hat or scarf. She could be hurt or frightened of the law, too. They might not ever locate her.

"We need to go home and get some sleep," he said, wishing they could have had better results. Wishing Emma didn't look so defeated. "I shouldn't have caused the wreck, but that would have been us if I hadn't taken action. The truck following us would have pushed us off the road and into a tree or embankment. Then they would have come after us and probably would have taken us or killed us on the spot."

"It's all right," Emma replied, her voice weary. "At least the girl got away. I hope she's okay."

"Maybe that picture you sent in can shed some light on who she is. I figure when the cruisers showed up at the accident scene, both parties made up quick explanations. They certainly wouldn't tell my own men that I was tailing them and they called in someone to run me off the road."

"But will they tell the police their real names?"

"I'm counting on it. Or that Pierce found something with one of the license plates, at least."

"Probably stolen or rented cars," Emma replied. "They seem to stay one step ahead of us."

"Well, we're getting closer," he said, remembering he hadn't told her the rest of the story. "Pierce matched some of the prints on that Dumpster."

She twisted in her seat. "Oh, that's right. You had some new information earlier. Spill it, Palladin."

Ryder took a deep breath. "Remember when you saw

that news report about a woman being attacked behind the Triple B?"

"Yes. I was that woman but they didn't mention my name."

"Right. And I figured someone had tipped off one of the local channels and they ran with the story?"

"Yes, I remember that businessman ranting about how Dallas needed to clean up that area of town."

"Yep. Well, funny thing. Pierce has video that could possibly place Bobby Doug Manchester at the Triple B the same night you were there. And one set of the prints they found on the Dumpster happens to match him, too."

Emma's expression changed from concerned to confused and shocked. "Are you telling me that Mr. Manchester could be involved in my assault and this investigation?"

"I'm telling you what we have. Proving it is gonna be a whole other can of worms."

"Let's open that can," she replied, a solid resolve overtaking her shock and weariness. "Let's get to it so I can find Reese. And if he is the one who has her, *he'll* be on the evening news very soon—and he'll be wearing handcuffs."

SEVENTEEN

They made it to the safe house, a cruiser escorting them across town. Ryder did a sweep of the place and deemed it all clear while Emma took in the two-bedroom apartment in a quiet subdivision just outside downtown. Wondering if Reese was out there somewhere, she stared out the living room windows at the glistening lights from the skyscrapers.

Until Ryder shut the blinds and curtains. "Don't stand at any of the windows."

"Right."

"We have a security system and the windows are hurricane strength. The front door is reinforced, too."

"So… I'm safe here?"

"As safe as anyone can be."

Plus, she had a hunky detective cowboy stalking around the perimeters of the apartment, too. Was she safe from him? Or rather, would her heart be safe *with* him?

She tried to acclimate herself with all the exits while he pulled out his phone to file a report about the smash-up and to check that the crime scene techs had received the photos Emma and he had managed to snap at the scene—both from the Triple B and the accident.

Emma took in the sliding doors to the small balcony,

an easy exit route if needed, and then stood staring at the empty fireplace, the hum of the air conditioner chilling her.

"Hey, you okay?" he asked from behind her.

Emma whirled and frowned at him. "I'm tired and worried and…I don't know…confused as to why a man like Bobby Doug Manchester would be involved in a smuggling ring, especially one that could include human trafficking."

"And why does that same man act so high and mighty in public, pontificating about crime when he could be one of the kingpins involved in that crime?"

"He's leading a double life," Emma replied. "He's hiding in plain sight because his ego won't allow him to be caught. He leaked my attack because he knew I must still be alive and then he ranted to the public and came to pay your department a visit. All good, believable covers for a man who has secrets. He likes toying with us, and he's probably the reason the locals botched finding Reese."

"I think you just answered your own question."

"I guess I did."

"Let's eat something and I'll start researching more online. It's too late to call Mildred tonight, but in the morning I'll plug in his name regarding the Triple B, and if we get a hit we might need to swing by and ask Mildred to help us dig a little more."

"You think he might be the silent owner?"

"I'd say he's a not-so-silent owner right now, but yes. My gut says he's up to his eyeballs in this." Ryder shot her a pointed glance. "If he was there the night you showed up, he must have had a good reason. Then he leaked your attack to the press so if anyone did come and finish you off, it would be hard to pin down who might have done it since half of Dallas heard about it."

"He'd blame the media and the police, of course." She held Ryder's gaze. "He might know where Reese is."

"I'm sure he knows because if we're right, he's trying to do some damage control. You threw a monkey wrench in his scheme."

Emma pushed at her tumbling hair and nodded, bile rising in her throat. "It's sickening but I agree with you. Why would he take Reese, though? Did Purdue see her and decide she'd fit the mold and so he just took her?"

She looked from him to the door. She needed air, needed to be out there. "I'm going to his house."

"No, you are not," Ryder said, turning to her. "Emma, it's understandable to want to confront him, but he's a dangerous man. If you do that, he'll kill you and then we'll never find Reese. You hear me?"

She shuddered, thinking about what Reese might be going through, that wall of panic closing in on her. "What if they took her away, Ryder? What if she's somewhere across the world in a strange country? I don't think I can take this."

He reached out, but Emma turned away again and wrapped her arms around her waist, trying to hold herself together, her eyes closed in a screaming prayer.

Lord, let her be safe and alive.

Ryder let out a breath and stepped away. He tapped his fingers on the small white counter that separated the kitchen from the living area. "I don't know. But if he has people like Brian Purdue doing his dirty work, he could easily take any girl he sets his eyes on."

"Don't talk about it," Emma said. "I can't stand the thought of what might happen to Reese if this man has her."

Ryder came back over to her and put his hands on her shoulders. "Emma, stay strong. We're getting closer every day. I'll put a rush on getting into Bobby Doug's business and I'll put people on him, night and day. It won't be easy since he has a lot of people in his pocket."

"Yes, which means he probably does have someone on the inside following us around."

"It looks that way. But you've got to stay put and stay close to me. Breathe, Emma. Take deep breaths."

Emma stared up at the man in front of her and did as he suggested. His strong hands steadied her and his eyes told her the things he couldn't say.

She reached up and touched his face. "Ryder, I'm so glad you're in this with me."

"I'll always be in this with you," he said. Then he lowered his head and kissed her, a brief touch that left her longing for more. But this time, he pulled away. "I'll make you something to eat."

He headed into the kitchen and took out sandwich meat and bread, his expression hard to read. How did he really feel about her? Was he fighting against this same attraction that had tugged at her since he'd walked into her hospital room?

He wasn't the settling-down kind. He had too much adrenaline in his system to settle down. She was the same way. They both worked in the shadows. When would they ever come into the light and find true happiness?

Emma was starving, but not for food. She was starving for a solid love, an unconditional love that would hold her and protect her and blanket her in hope and peace and contentment.

The kind of love where strong hands steadied her and made her feel worthy and family stayed tight-knit and close and made her feel as if she belonged.

I will not leave you comfortless. She thought about the Scriptures and knew she could count on God to see her through. But she wanted to count on Ryder, too. Could she allow herself to dream about such things?

No. Not until she knew Reese was safe. She'd come here for that purpose, and she intended to finish the job, no matter what. No matter that Ryder's kisses belied his moods. No matter that her heart was getting too far ahead of her brain.

Ryder brought over a tray with two sandwiches and some fruit and chips. "Emma, come on and eat."

She sat down at the small bistro table across from the tiny fireplace, her stomach too jittery for food. "Thank you."

Ryder handed her a glass of tea. "I'm wondering if we should go back over the list of Reese's friends. See if any name stands out."

Emma lifted her head, her mouth dropping open. "Ryder, the Parkers moved from Houston to Dallas."

"Yes, we know that."

"They moved and found a good school district, but Reese only went to that school for about year. Then they moved into a different, more private neighborhood and put her in an exclusive private school. Why? Do you think that could have something to do with someone taking her?"

He looked confused. "People change schools all the time and the Parkers can certainly afford to send her to a private school, but I guess that does seem abrupt."

Emma took a sip of tea. "I just find it odd that they loved the school she was in and then they moved her to this other school, practically on the other side of the city." She put down her half-eaten sandwich. "A private, gated neighborhood and a private school."

Ryder's eyes widened. "They were trying to protect her."

"But from who or what? What are they not telling us?"

"We need to go back and visit her parents, Emma."

"Yes, we sure do."

"We need a list of her friends from both schools," he said. "Maybe one of those friends can explain the sudden change."

"Or maybe one of those friends knows *why* the sudden change happened but isn't talking. I need to pin down Tessa Clark. We also need to try to compare the one photo I snapped of that girl with her. If that was Tessa, I hope she got away and is safe at least."

He gave her an admiring glance. "We have our work cut out for us, but I'm beginning to think we'll have our answers soon."

Emma sat with her hands in her lap, her heart risking hope. "And that I'll find Reese before it's too late."

Ryder reached across the space separating them and she lifted her hand to his. "Let's pray that we're on the right track. Eat up while I call this in, but only to Pierce for now. We've got a long night ahead of us."

Emma held tight to his hand. "She has to be okay, Ryder."

"I know," he said, dropping her hand. "I know that's what you're hoping."

Emma saw the doubt in his expression and heard it in his words. "But you're not so sure, right?"

"I want to be sure," he said, "but with this new revelation, we have to face the possibility that it might already be too late."

"You mean I have to face that possibility?"

"We both know how these situations can go bad, Emma. You need to be prepared."

"I won't give up," Emma said, anger and disappointment in her words. "Even if you already have."

Then she got up and hurried into the bedroom and shut the door while she had herself a good cry.

"Emma?"

Ryder knocked on the door again.

She wasn't responding.

"Emma, say something so I'll know you're okay."

He heard noises. Water running in the bathroom, the closet door slamming. But she wasn't talking.

He had to go and say it, didn't he? He knew better, but she was on a roller-coaster ride of sheer agony and he wanted her to consider this case as she would any other, by looking at all the worst possible scenarios and varying outcomes.

But this one was tough.

"I'm sorry," he said, his hand on the door, his heart in there with her. "I'm so sorry. We won't give up. I told you I'll be here with you in this, no matter what. You've got to believe that, okay?"

The door opened on such a swift shift of air he almost fell through, but he caught himself. Then he looked into her red-rimmed, swollen eyes. He'd made her cry.

"Emma…"

She fell against him. "I don't want this. I don't. I don't want to be here. I don't want her to be out there. I want her alive and safe and behind closed gates, if that's what it takes. I can't move beyond that." Pulling away, she glared at him, anger overcoming her despair. "Don't ever say that to me again."

"I won't," he said, a promise he aimed to keep. "I won't."

Because he never wanted to hurt her or see that horrible anguish in her eyes again.

She nodded and then shut the door. "Go to sleep, Ryder," she said loud enough for him to hear. "Just go to sleep."

"I'm not sleeping," he retorted, his words just as loud. "I'm going to search until I have answers."

The door swung open again. "So am I. Where do we start?"

Ryder admired her spunk and her spirit. She had guts and tenacity. She was more woman than he'd ever had to handle before, more of a challenge than he'd ever dreamed a woman could be. She confused him, questioned him, kept up with him and moved ahead of him.

He was in too deep, and that scared him.

But he couldn't stand the thought of watching her walk away.

"Let's start *over* and stay focused on what we both want," he said, not telling that he really just wanted to take her into his arms and hold her close. "You want to find Reese. I do, too. But I also want to bring down this ring of criminals. The two are connected, but we have to put that connection together or we could mess up the whole thing."

"Agreed."

Ryder took her by the hand and brought her back to the table where he'd set up camp with his laptop and phone and what few electronic files he'd pulled up.

Then he made a pot of coffee and told her to write out a list of Reese's school friends, from the old and new school. And he also told her to make a list of the people in the Parkers' inner circle. Because there could be a distinct possibility that the Parkers and Bobby Doug Manchester moved in the same circles.

Ryder rubbed his eyes and looked over at the woman sleeping on the couch. Emma had found a lot of details regarding Bobby Doug Manchester and his wife Sabrina but she'd become so exhausted he'd made her lie down for a few minutes.

That had been around two o'clock in the morning and now it was close to dawn. She had fallen asleep and hadn't moved very much since he'd covered her with a light blanket.

But they had a solid list of both Reese's friends, based on her social media accounts, and of the people the Parkers associated with, according to the social pages and several online photos of them at charity gatherings.

In one of those photos, the Parkers stood dressed in formal attire and smiling into the cameras, alongside Bobby Doug and Sabrina Manchester. The photo had been taken about a year ago at a big charity event held in a downtown hotel.

"They sure look chummy."

Ryder glanced up to find Emma standing behind him, her eyes still sleepy, her hair tousled and tumbling. He had to fight the urge to pull her into his arms and kiss her again.

"Yeah. But this was a while back. The Manchesters have three children, two boys and a girl. The girl is the same age as Reese."

Emma's sleepiness cleared away. She leaned down to stare at the family picture on Bobby Doug's business site.

"A family affair," she read from the caption. "His wife looks like the cat that swallowed the canary. A bit too catty for me," Emma noted.

"Yes, Sabrina Manchester is the consummate socialite— the kind that serves on the board for things like the Cattleman's Ball and the cotillion. The list of their charitable causes is impressive, and so is the article I found that shows a complete tour of their mansion."

"I need coffee," Emma said. "What's the girl's name?"

"Sarabeth," he replied, watching her.

Emma whirled from the coffeepot. "Did you say Sarabeth?"

"Yes."

She came over with a fresh cup, her hands wrapped around the mug. "She's on the list from the old school."

"I noticed that," Ryder said, getting up to stretch. "And she works at the country club from the old neighborhood."

"Which I'm guessing is where the Manchester estate is located."

"Yes. So the Parkers moved from a pretty secure, upscale neighborhood to yet another, even more secure and exclusive subdivision."

"I wonder if Sarabeth is working today."

"We can't approach his daughter, Emma. He'd come after us hard on that one."

"Then what do you suggest we do first? I feel like I'm going around in circles."

"Let's go talk to the Parkers."

"Okay." She started toward her room. "I need to freshen up."

"Take your time. It's only five in the morning."

Emma pivoted back. "Why did you let me sleep so long, Ryder?"

"Because you needed to rest."

She didn't argue with him. "Thank you. I'm going to get a shower and then find some breakfast."

"Okay, and after the sun is fully in the sky, you can call the Parkers and ask if we can come by."

She nodded. "I don't think they'll mind. I'm sure they're beside themselves with worry, so anything we can do to help will give them a glimmer of hope."

She stopped, her hand on the doorjamb. "I don't want to give them false hope, but we need to find out what they know about the Manchesters."

Ryder hated the defeat in her words. "We will. And Emma, this is better than shifting in the wind, right?"

"Yes. The closer we get to the truth, the sooner we can find Reese."

Ryder prayed that would be so. But he didn't voice his concerns. He'd learned his lesson on that. So while he waited for Emma, he went back over the information he'd gathered and called Pierce to give him a report.

"We're getting there," he told his partner.

"Yeah. I'll try to see if I can pull up Manchester's phone records. Now that we have him as possibly being at the scene, I think we're within our rights to do so."

"Just be careful. He has deep pockets. I think someone on the inside is reporting to him."

Pierce didn't speak right away. "I never considered that until you mentioned it, but you're right about the sheriff's department where they live. Not too keen on handing over information or telling me what they did find."

"Well, consider it now since Manchester could be lining their pockets," Ryder replied. "And watch your back."

After he ended the call, he had to wonder. Did Pierce know something he didn't? Was Pierce on his side, or could his partner be setting a trap for them?

EIGHTEEN

Emma finished her coffee while she gathered clean clothes, memories pouring over her like hard pebbles, dreams coming back to frighten her. But this was no dream. This was a real-life nightmare that seemed to be playing out in a slow, horrible way.

She showered and dressed in a hurry, wearing jeans and a black T-shirt, her hair air-drying as she tidied her room and checked her phone. No calls from Tessa Clark. She'd try the girl's number again. Over and over until she heard from her.

Last night, Emma and Ryder had gathered headshots from social media sources of as many of Reese's friends as they could find. Those social apps sure came in handy when trying to track people down.

But they'd found nothing unusual on Reese's social pages. Just the obligatory selfies with smiles and antics. No pictures to connect her to either Tessa or the Manchester's daughter, Sarabeth, either.

Had those two been her friends, or had she removed them from her online photo albums?

Emma shook out her hair and checked her lip gloss. She'd lost weight and she needed a tan, but right now, neither of those things mattered. So she opened the door and found Ryder sitting at the bistro table reading over files.

"Coffee's fresh," he said, not even looking up. "I made a new pot."

Like her, beyond reporting things, he obviously wasn't a morning person.

"Thank you."

Emma decided they were doing some kind of dance. A ritual that drew them in and then tugged them apart. Neither of them wanted to be here together, but then again, they seemed to work great together if they each focused on what they wanted to accomplish. But as far as being two human beings who needed each other, not so much. They couldn't voice that kind of need.

Better to keep fighting the good fight.

And pray that they'd win.

"I found a picture of Tessa Clark," Ryder said, lifting his gaze to hit Emma square in the face. His eyes wandered over her, warming her and chilling her, and saying things she wasn't ready to hear.

Emma cleared her head. "Let me see."

She looked at the computer screen and then pulled up the photo she'd taken in the dark last night. "Same blond hair and same height as the girl last night, but we never got a good look at her face."

Ryder shut the laptop. "But I'm guessing it's her and that's why she's not returning your calls."

"I could have put her in danger, too," Emma said. "Now we have two missing girls."

Ryder downed the rest of his coffee and stood. "Let's get back to the courthouse and see what we can find on this deed. I've got Pierce and two trusted officers working on some other things. Oh, by the way, the two cars involved in the crash didn't bring us any good news. Rentals through a corporation and since both parties claim it was an accident and we can't prove they aren't the people they say they are, we got nothing to pin on them." He took a swig of coffee. "Of course, they never mentioned anyone else being involved."

"So these henchmen are obviously professionals. That's an upgrade from the shooter out at the ranch."

"Yes, but the heat is on. They'll probably be replaced yet again."

"But the lawyer got away," Emma reminded him. "We know those two men came out of the bar right before he did."

"They claim they had business and met there—for the barbecue. Said they don't know John Clayton. We can't match them to him. None of them mentioned the girl."

"This is a game of cat and mouse," Emma said. "They don't know what we know and we can't guess what they're doing."

"Yep."

His refusal to look at her didn't go unnoticed. Brooding. Maybe he regretted holding her and reassuring her. Maybe he didn't want that kind of burden in his life. She knew the feeling.

They'd worked together into the wee hours, but Emma sensed a distance between them—a protection mechanism, she decided. She should know. She'd been using that tactic for most of her adult life. Her heart and her faith had become broken after she found herself pregnant and alone. She'd turned back to God because her heart couldn't take the pain all on its own. But Emma had never truly forgiven herself.

Now, she didn't think she deserved the kind of life that brought stability and contentment. If Reese wasn't okay, Emma would never find any kind of contentment and peace.

Ryder checked the parking lot and the unmarked vehicle they were using. "All good," he said.

Soon they were back in the county clerk's office. Mildred greeted them with what might be called a smile. Close anyway.

"I found a name," she said without preamble.

"Oh, really?" Ryder's smile beamed in spite of his grumpy mood earlier. "Let's hear it."

Mildred proceeded to show them on the computer screen. "The building belongs to a corporation—SAM Enterprises."

"Sam?" Emma squinted at the file. "Who is Sam?"

"It's probably an acronym," Mildred pointed out. "Someone's initials maybe."

SAM.

Emma glanced at Ryder, but his expression was unreadable. After he'd thanked Mildred and they had copies of what they needed, they got back in the car.

"What?" Emma asked him.

"What do you mean, what?"

"What are you thinking?"

"SAM is the acronym for the corporation listed on the rental cars. They used a corporate credit card."

"So the same people who own the bar also rented the car we were tailing and the one that tailed us?"

He shrugged and hit the gas after the traffic light changed. "The *M* could stand for Manchester."

Emma nodded. "I thought that, too. Could the *S* stand for Sabrina?"

"His wife's name? Maybe."

"The *A* could be one of their middle initials or her maiden name."

"It has to be a shell corporation."

"Makes sense to me," she replied. Then she looked at her watch. "I'm going to try Tessa again, and the Parkers are expecting us at ten o'clock." She'd called them on the way out this morning and told them she needed to ask some more questions.

Ryder slanted his gaze at her. "Okay. Later today, we need to question Brian Purdue again. Maybe drop a few names and rattle him."

"Good idea." She liked the way he'd said "we." They'd held Purdue for outstanding warrants in another county and used paperwork to stall things, but he'd be a free man soon enough if they didn't pin him down on something that could stick.

"So John Clayton hasn't paid Purdue's bail yet since the judge set it so high. But he did visit him once. Do you think to help him or threaten him?"

"A little of both, but mostly threats, I think," Ryder said. "Probably coming from the top."

"You mean from Bobby Doug?"

"Yes."

They made it across town and drove the interstate for a few miles before Ryder pulled the car off onto an exit that led to a big subdivision surrounded by quaint shops and a swanky golf course. Emma gave him the code to get them in the main gate since it was now kept shut at all times.

Ryder was jittery this morning. He'd had too much caffeine and too much time to think about how this woman had turned his world upside down. Then he'd taken out his feelings on the one person who didn't need anything else thrown at her.

He didn't like this quiet between them. He'd rather she

spar with him and try to outthink him. They worked professionally…but personally, they were both all over the map.

One more reason to avoid these feelings that kept getting into the way.

"The coffee shop is in that little strip mall," she said, pointing to a turn-in to the right in front of the black, iron-barred fence surrounding the subdivision. "The kids apparently come and go, using a code to open the gate. Reese took that short route to head home."

"But Purdue got to her before she made it through the gate?"

Emma closed her eyes, took a breath. "Yes. The Parkers and the neighborhood HOA are demanding more cameras around the perimeters of the property."

"Good idea," Ryder replied. "I read through some of the reports and saw where they'd sent out search-and-rescue volunteers with K-9s right after she went missing."

"Yes, but they didn't find anything beyond the spot by the gate. That led the police to believe she was taken away in a vehicle."

"That would be the assumption if the K-9s alerted on that spot."

"And I saw the video of Purdue pulling out of that same parking lot. The locals never even considered asking for surveillance video. They mishandled the whole case. That's why the Parkers called me."

"Well," Ryder said, his tone softening, his hand touching lightly on her for a split second, "we're on the case now. And we're getting closer and closer to the truth."

Emma took one last glance toward the fancy strip mall. "Yes, but I want to get to Reese."

They went through the open gate and Ryder turned left based on the GPS. "Nice digs."

"The school is just past the golf course," Emma said,

her eyes wide as they passed huge, rambling mansions with manicured, sloping lawns. "I could have never given Reese this kind of life."

Seeing the pain in her eyes and hearing the disappointment in her words, Ryder tried to reassure her. "Hey, you do okay. You have your own business and you're a hard worker."

"Yes, but I'm gone for days at a time and I barely make ends meet. Not to mention dealing with all sorts of tricky situations." Staring ahead, she added, "I live in a two-bedroom beach house and have a heavy mortgage. This... is not what I would have expected, but I wanted her to have a good family. How can I be sure now that she does have all the things I dreamed of for her? She's supposed to be better off here."

Ryder didn't argue with her. Now was not the time.

Emma let out a sigh. "Or at least, I thought she was better off here. We have to find out what the Parkers are not telling us."

Ryder pulled into the long circular drive in front of the Parkers' two-storied brick-and-stone mansion. "Wow."

"Yes." Emma stared up at the portico. "The last time I was here it was late and I was exhausted. I barely paid attention to my surroundings. This is impressive, but I'll be searching for clues instead of admiring the artwork and architectural details."

"I'll be right there with you," Ryder said, meaning in more ways than one. He planned to keep his promise to her. He'd see this through until the bitter end, regardless of his mixed emotions. Because Emma would need someone there at the end, either way.

They went up to the massive door and Ryder hit the doorbell. "Here we go."

Emma took in deep breaths and nodded, but he could tell she was fighting her panic.

Annette Parker opened the door, her smile tight, her eyes red-rimmed and shadowed by dark circles of fatigue. "Come in, Emma, Detective Palladin."

Emma hugged Annette close. "I wish we had good news, but we are making progress. We need more information."

Annette's chin lifted in acknowledgment. "Joseph is waiting in the den. I have coffee and muffins. The neighbors keep bringing food. Some of them are still making the rounds with posters and search parties. We have to hold out hope."

Ryder's gaze met Emma's. They all needed to hold out hope. He'd been wrong to tell Emma otherwise.

They followed her up a wide hallway with marble floors and fancy rugs and turned right into a spacious den that overlooked a swimming pool and the golf course beyond.

Joseph stood at the floor-to-ceiling windows, his back turned. The man looked broken and aged.

"Joseph?" Annette's voice cracked. "Emma's here with Detective Palladin."

Joseph turned and came forward, extending his hand to Emma. "We appreciate everything you've done. Any news?"

"No," Emma said, her eyes misty. "But we've had some new developments and we need to ask you both a few questions."

"Let's sit down," Joseph said, motioning to a white leather sofa with two matching chairs across from it.

Annette served coffee and placed the muffins and fruit on the table. No one took any of the food.

"So, do you know Bobby Doug Manchester?" Ryder

asked without preamble, hoping to gauge the couple's re-
action.

Annette lowered her eyes and fidgeted with her pearls.
Joseph cleared his throat and adjusted his glasses.

Emma glanced from Ryder to the couple. "We need to
know everything. If you want me to find Reese, you need
to tell me anything that could give us a clue or a lead."

"We knew them, yes," Joseph said. "But I'm not sure
what knowing the Manchesters has to do with Reese not
being here."

The man couldn't voice that his daughter was missing,
Ryder noted.

"Did Reese know their daughter, Sarabeth?" Ryder
asked, his gaze scanning the room. Just a normal, over-
done straight-out-of-a-magazine kind of place. Sterile and
perfectly decorated. A huge portrait of a steam cargo boat
chugging up the Trinity River spotlighted over the fireplace, the water and trees so vibrant and colorful they
looked real.

But something was missing here. Warmth. The place
lacked warmth.

The coldness wrapped around Ryder, gripping him like
a wet cloak.

"Reese and Sarabeth were friends before," Annette finally said.

"You mean, before you moved here and put Reese in
the private school down the road?" Emma asked, her tone
firm.

"Yes." Annette bobbed her head, her blond hair thick
and shining. "But…they had some sort of falling-out."

Emma took a breath. "Did Reese seem okay with that?"

Annette glanced at her husband, seeking permission
maybe?

"She changed after they had their big fight. She grew

more moody and quiet. Depressed. But she wouldn't tell us what was wrong. All we knew was that Sarabeth had confronted her in front of a lot of people and they'd had words."

Joseph took a sip of coffee. "We talked to doctors and therapists, but they said she was fine. Just teenaged angst. Then she asked about going to another school."

"So you gave her what she wanted?" Ryder asked. "You moved into this subdivision?"

"We did what we thought best," Annette replied, her blue eyes wide, her tone defensive. "She was so miserable. We thought maybe Sarabeth was harassing her. She'd picked on Tessa—the girl I mentioned who called me the morning after Reese went missing. Reese had come to Tessa's defense, so we thought maybe that was the reason for the fight and the possible harassment."

"Bullying?" Emma asked.

"We didn't call it that. Just mean-girl kind of stuff." Annette held to her pearls.

"Bullying," Ryder repeated. "So once you moved here, did Reese change, get better?"

"Yes," Annette said "But she was never the same. She was happier here and liked school, made new friends. She and Tessa stayed friends. Tessa was there with her that day but left early." She stopped, put her hands together. "I wish we'd never allowed Reese to walk home that day. I mean, it was a half mile from here. Just outside the gates. I wish we'd never moved here either. She might be safe if we'd stayed where we were."

"But the Manchesters lived in that neighborhood," Emma said. "You felt you had to get away, take Reese out of that mean-girl situation?"

Joseph stood, his hands fisting. "What do you know, Miss Langston? Do you think the Manchesters had something to do with Reese being taken?"

NINETEEN

Emma met Joseph Parker's anger head-on. "Why don't you tell me that, sir? Everything you've told us here today could have helped early on if we'd known about it."

"We didn't think that had anything to do with this," Annette said, tears in her eyes. "We were past that and the Manchesters didn't know where we'd moved. Sarabeth stopped bothering Reese once we moved."

Her husband went to her and took her into his arms, then looked over at Ryder and Emma. "This has been a tremendous stress on our lives. Our daughter is missing and we've been trying to find her for two weeks now. We've been questioned, scrutinized, condemned and re-deemed. We've had interviews with the local authorities who botched this and the Dallas police and even the FBI. We truly thought Reese had been kidnapped. How could we even imagine that people we used to socialize with might be at the center of this?"

Emma went over and sat by Annette and took her hand. "We have reason to believe that Bobby Doug might be involved, but we don't have anything concrete for evidence yet. So you have to stay calm and if you hear anything from the Manchesters, we need to know, okay? We're not accusing you or them of anything. We're just trying to put together the pieces."

Annette wiped at her eyes. "I should have questioned Reese more about Sarabeth. They were close, but we only saw Sarabeth's parents at social events. They were a bit brash to us, but we were always polite since our daughter was friends with their daughter. But I can assure you we don't know anything beyond that." Turning to her husband, she started crying again. "Why didn't we try to find out what really happened? I can't believe we were so naive and clueless."

Reese shook her head. "Parents don't always know what to do with teenagers who hide things. You moved Reese out of a bad situation, so be glad of that. The information we have might mean nothing, but we had to ask. And you've helped us by being honest. Now we can focus closer to home and see if this development brings us anything we can use."

Ryder stood, his notebook in his hand. "It's important that you don't discuss what we've told you with anyone. One rumor could sink our whole investigation."

"And put Reese in even more danger," Emma added, hoping they'd listen.

"We won't say a word," Annette replied. "We won't risk that, I can promise you."

Joseph stood with both of them. "I won't repeat anything, but I'm telling you both, if I find out Bobby Doug harmed Reese in any way, I can't promise what will happen then."

Emma stood toe-to-toe with the distraught father. "Don't worry, Joseph, you won't have to lift a finger. I'll be the one to take care of him if that's the case."

Ryder took her by the arm, but Annette stood and rushed to Emma. "I know how difficult this is for you," she said, tears streaming down her face. "If—when we find Reese, I want to tell her the truth about you. She should know what you've sacrificed for her. Especially this."

Emma blinked back tears. "Let's find her first and then we'll decide what to do about everything else."

The Parkers walked them to the door.

"Stay safe," Annette said. "We'll be here doing what we can. We won't give up."

"I won't either," Emma said. "Call if you hear anything, and I'll do the same."

When they were back in the car, she turned to stare out the window, the opulence of this place so overwhelming that she wanted to break glass. "All the fences and alarms in the world, and she gets nabbed right outside this sanctuary. Someone knew her routine, Ryder, same as they know ours."

Ryder turned into the parking lot of the strip mall. "*Someone knew her routine.* And her friends all had somewhere to be that afternoon. They left her. Tessa was one of those friends."

Emma's heart lurched. Sitting up, she stared at the coffee shop. "Do you think Tessa was in on this from the beginning?"

Ryder's grim expression told her what she needed to know. "It's pure speculation, but we need to find Tessa Clark and clear up a few things. Did she and the others leave Reese alone on purpose? And if that was Tessa we saw with the men last night, did they force her into this? Or is she one of them, a willing participant?"

"But she called Annette after Reese went missing."

"She would. I mean, if she's pretending to be Reese's best friend. Or if someone threatened her to be their accomplice, she might have had a pang of guilt and decided to confess."

"And now she's running scared again," Emma finished. "This is worse than I ever imagined."

"We've got to keep at it," Ryder said. "Until we have the truth, we can't bring them all down."

Emma pointed to the coffee shop. "So let's start right here. The manager knows all the local kids. Maybe he can shed some light on how they were acting that day. I questioned him once, but he didn't have much to offer. But if I go at it from a different angle, he might remember something important."

"He or anyone else who was here that day, too," Ryder replied. "I could use a good cup of coffee and a doughnut. How about you?"

"Coffee, yes. Doughnut, probably not. My stomach is roiling with anxiety right now."

Ryder hit the steering wheel. "I'm sorry. I didn't think about how hard this has been for you, being back here yet again. I'll go in and ask questions and you can wait here."

She nodded. "That's a good idea. I need some time to think about all of this." She opened her door. "I'm going to walk the parking lot, blow off some of this angst."

"Be careful," he said, glancing around. "I'll be right inside and I'll have one eye on you."

"I'll be okay," she replied. "I mean what could happen? Somebody in a blue truck coming by to grab me?"

"That's not funny, Emma."

"I'm not laughing."

With that she got out and took off toward the spot where Emma had been taken, all the while praying that some kind of clue would emerge or that she'd remember something important.

Dear Lord, we need Your help now more than ever. Each minute is precious. Show us the way and lead us on the right path.

Emma strolled around the perimeter of the area, the hot summer sun burning through her clothes. While her heart burned with the need to find Reese.

Maybe then she'd be able to put her own life on the right path, too, wherever that road might lead her. From the way he waffled in the love department, she didn't think that path would lead her to Ryder Palladin.

She checked the turnoff toward the closed gate, made sure no cars were lurking off the main road. Then she scanned the parking lot. Several vehicles, but all looked empty. But then, anyone could be watching her right now.

Emma welcomed a confrontation. "Bring it."

But no one came after her. The afternoon was ominously quiet. No wind lifted through the tall pines and old oaks. No vehicle came barreling toward her. She moved through the shallow, grassy ditch a few yards from the black iron-railed gate, wondering if Reese had walked these steps. Emma kicked at the grass, glad it hadn't rained in a while. Then she spotted what looked like a white plastic grocery bag.

Hurrying to it, Emma found a long stick of bramble and lifted the bag into the air. "Trash," she said, disappointment moving through her. But then she noticed something inside the bag. A plastic drinking cup with the Blue Bull Bar logo on it. A charging, mad blue bull, his wild black eyes staring up at her and the words *The Blue Bull Bar. Barbecue and Ribs, Beer and Spirits. Friends and Rebels.*

Glancing around, Emma saw Ryder coming toward her with two to-go cups of coffee. "Ready?"

Emma brought the bag to him, holding it on the thick foot-long twig like a hobo bag. "Yes. Ryder, I found something in the tall grass."

Ryder peered inside and immediately saw the cup. "Hmm. Now that's interesting. How did anyone miss this?"

"We don't know if it's been here since that day, but if it has I think it stayed hidden behind grass and leaves. But the bag is intact and there is a possibility the DNA inside could be protected. It hasn't rained in three weeks. This cup could tell us a lot, don't you think?"

"Yes." He handed her one of the coffees. "Let me take it and put it in an evidence bag. Should be some in the trunk."

Emma followed him to the car, a shiver moving down her spine. They could be watching Ryder and her right now. "Did you find out anything inside?"

"A few details," he said. "We'll talk once we head back to the office."

They got inside the car and Emma took a sip of her coffee. "That bag is full of trash. But that cup means someone from the Triple B was here, just like the bumper sticker on the truck brought me to the Triple B. I didn't see the bag last time I looked, but I didn't go down into the ditch either."

Ryder watched the road and checked in the rearview mirror. "If that trash was in the blue truck, Purdue wouldn't have been stupid enough to throw it out near where he took Reese."

Emma looked at Ryder, hope blooming again in her heart. "No, but Reese could have been smart enough to kick it out the door when he forced her into that truck."

Ryder nodded. "She would hope someone would find it. A long shot but, yes, a smart move." His gaze moved over Emma. "She obviously takes after her mother."

Emma couldn't speak. Her heart hammered a cadence inside her pulse. The bag of trash could be from another vehicle, or it could have fallen out of the truck in the chaos of Reese being taken. But Emma had to hope Reese had risked shoving that bag of trash out to save herself. To give her hope that the area would be searched and some-one would find that bag and go through it.

Help us, Lord. Help us the way You helped me today.

Emma held to her silent prayer.

Then she felt Ryder's hand on hers. "We'll head back to the ranch and regroup."

"No. We have to keep moving, Ryder. What did you find out from the manager?"

"He told me that Reese used to come in a lot and, yes, Tessa was with her most of the time. He remembered both of them. He said Tessa seemed shy and quiet and Reese was bubbly and kind."

Emma's eyes misted over. "But nothing else."

"No."

"We need to find Tessa."

"You're exhausted and this has been a hard day. Let me take you to the ranch just for an overnight stay. I can work from there. I'll call Pierce and fill him in on everything we've found, too. He never leaves the station anyway."

Emma wondered about that. "Can you trust him?"

The words were out before she could take them back, but Emma was beyond being discreet.

Ryder's eyebrow winged up, surprise darkening his eyes. "Do *you* trust him?"

"He was there that night, Ryder. He found me and then he called you, right?"

"Right. But if he was in cahoots with anyone, he could have finished the job himself and blamed them."

"Or he could pretend to help me because he knew you would come looking and that they'd kill him if he didn't do something quick."

Ryder shook his head. "Look, I've worked with Pierce Daughtry for a couple of years and he's never been any-thing but loyal to the Dallas PD. He's worked to bring down some of the worst criminals in this city. The man is like a bulldog on crime. I can't see him doing something like this."

"I'm sorry," she said, "but he has all the information that you and I have. He's known where we are just about every minute."

"Yes, he knew we were at the safe house last night and nothing happened there."

"Too hot," she said. "Too risky."

"Emma, stop." Ryder stared ahead, but she could see the anger coming off him like fumes. "Stop grasping at straws. I can't believe Pierce would do that. He's not the kind of man to hit a woman, let alone try to kill one."

"Then who is? Who within your department would be a mole for Bobby Doug Manchester?"

Ryder's dark scowl didn't help matters. "I don't know, but to prove you wrong, I'll add that to the list of things I need to look into." Then he gunned the engine. "But until then, you're coming back to the ranch with me tonight. You need to be out of the city of Dallas right now."

"Fair enough," she said, too tired for a battle even if she did feel like he was trying to bulldoze her. "And Ryder, I'm not grasping at straws. I'm trying to decipher every angle and every scenario."

"I understand," he retorted, "but you have to trust *me* sooner or later. And right now, I don't see that happening."

"That works both ways, Palladin," she replied. "You have major trust issues, too. I can't decide if it's because a woman did a number on you or because you think you have to save the world."

"I can save the world as long as I don't have a woman in my life," he retorted. "So let's just get on with this."

TWENTY

Emma stayed silent on the drive out to the ranch. Ryder had a reason to be angry with her, but she had lots of reasons to suspect everyone around him. But she didn't think this new anger stemmed from her doubting his partner.

No, the man was trying his level best to push her away because he thought no woman could handle his dangerous career.

And she didn't have any inclination of convincing him.

So that was that. All that chemistry and steam between them would just go up in a puff of relief when this was over. Fine by her.

Now they were focusing on the locals in Wood Hills. After they'd left the strip mall by the gate, Ryder had driven to the small station that worked under the jurisdiction of the sheriff's department. He and Emma had talked to two officers, a young female rookie named Rhonda Harper who'd been on the force two years and an older captain who insisted they'd done everything they could to help locate the girl.

"The whole community got involved but we ran dry."

The captain seemed sincere but Rhonda grew angry.

"The girl walked off by herself. She told the others she

had to go home. It's tragic but we think she ran away. You might want to question her parents a little more."

Emma now thought about the woman's attitude. Rhonda seemed confident and sure and she was a pretty woman who worked in a man's world. Maybe she wanted to do more but hadn't been able to get past the big boys.

"I'm wondering about Rhonda Harper," she said, hoping to lull Ryder out of his dark mood.

"Just like you're wondering about everyone else who works in law enforcement in and around Dallas, right?"

"Are you going to hold that over my head from here out?" she asked as dusk scattered around them.

"I might." He let out a tired sigh. "I understand why you'd be suspicious, but I trust everyone I work with. Our department is clean. I can't speak for other divisions, however."

"So you did pick up on the vibes today?"

"Yes. Rhonda was a tad too defensive. I think she's hiding something."

"Can we do a check on her?"

"Of course. Already working on it."

Darkness had fallen when they pulled up to the ranch house.

"So we go inside just as we always do," Ryder said. "Then when we have the all clear later tonight, we move you to the cabin. Spur will go with us. He's a good guard dog."

Emma didn't argue. She was exhausted and still no closer to finding Reese.

She reached for her door handle but Ryder stopped her. "Something's not right. Where's Spur?"

Emma glanced at the house. It was dark. "Maybe your mom's not home. Maybe Spur's with her."

"No, I checked with her an hour ago."

Emma could feel the tension in the air. The porch lights weren't on, nor were the security lights.

"Ryder?"

"Listen to me," he said. "You know the way to the cabin. I want you to get out and run there as fast as you can, understand?"

"No. I won't leave you."

"Emma, do as I say. Go through the back woods same as you did the other day when we had the breach in security." He handed her his weapon. "Use this. It has a full magazine of fifteen rounds." He gave her a numbered code to open the cabin. "When you get inside, lock up and reset the alarm, okay?"

"What are you going to do?" she asked, her heart bursting with anger and fear.

"I'm going to call for backup and then I'm going to check the house." He leaned close. "If you see anyone you don't recognize, shoot them."

Emma nodded but she had no intention of leaving him and his family alone. "All right. Call me when it's clear."

"I will." His gaze held hers. "Emma…"

He didn't finish the sentence. He tugged her close and kissed her with a force that left her heart wanting more and her mind whirling with anxiety.

Then he nodded. "Go to the cabin and wait for me."

Emma got out and took one last look at him, then carefully made her way around the house, the heavy gun giving her courage.

The bunkhouse was dark, too, but she decided to check there for any intruders. Her heart bumped warnings with each step and each snap of a twig. She could see the cabin in the moonlight. If she headed there, she'd be safe.

But Ryder wouldn't. What about his mother and sister?

She went to the bunkhouse, thinking she could hide

there until she heard from Ryder. When she peeked through the window, she saw a man sitting in a chair. Another man lay on the floor.

Emma didn't hesitate. She opened the door and burst into the room, her gun drawn.

The man in the chair had a cloth gag around his mouth and his hands tied behind his back, but his eyes widened at the sight of her gun. Emma hurried to take off the gag. "What happened?"

"We heard shooting. Two went to investigate and I came in here and found Will shot. Someone grabbed me and tied me up and gagged me. I never saw their face."

"Take care of Will," she said, deciding she wouldn't hide out here or at the cabin. "I'm going to find Ryder and the others. Help is on the way."

The man bobbed his head and went to his friend. "Be careful," he said. "He was mad and loaded for bear. I think he might have done something to Spur, too."

Emma made it to the house with every sound and crunch upping her anxiety, her breath coming in huffs, a wave of dizziness overcoming her. Taking in air, she tried to focus, but vertigo seemed to be pulling her into a vortex. Why now? She had exerted herself too much and aggravated her confused brain? Or her panic attacks were coming back full force? She had to keep going, her mind on getting to the house to help Ryder.

She trotted in a crouch toward the back door and immediately noticed it was slightly open. Careful to stay quiet, she blinked back her dizziness and took another breath before she slipped inside.

Just breathe. Just breathe.

Emma made it inside the house.

"Stop right there, lady."

* * *

Ryder edged around the garage, praying that Emma had made it to the cabin. He'd called Sheriff Watson of the local police, but it would take a while for anyone to come to their rescue. The front door was jammed, so he couldn't get it unlocked. He didn't dare open the garage. That would make too much noise.

The back door was his only option.

He moved toward it, sweat pouring off his brow and down his backbone. When he spotted a figure moving toward the door from the other direction, he recognized Emma. Then he heard the creak of a footstep behind him.

Something hard slammed against his head, and Ryder went down. Then the world went black.

Emma turned toward the kitchen and found a grizzly man holding a gun to Stephanie's rib cage. "Don't come any farther or I'll shoot her and you."

Emma nodded and held her hands up, her gaze moving from him to Stephanie and then all around the room. "Okay. It's cool."

"No, it's not," he said. "Put down that weapon and get over here. You're a lot of trouble, woman."

Emma didn't argue with him, but she wanted to scream out Ryder's name. Laying her gun on the floor, she gave Stephanie what she hoped was a reassuring look. "It's going to all work out," she said, wondering where Nancy was and if she was all right.

Stephanie's frightened gaze slanted to behind the counter.

Emma did a quick glance and saw a booted foot. Nancy was on the floor and she wasn't moving. Had this man shot her and Ryder?

"Shove it over here," the man said, holding Stephanie as a shield.

What happened next took all of them by surprise.

Emma shoved the gun toward the man with a hard, deliberate push. It went past him and landed behind the counter. He looked over just long enough to give Stephanie a chance to elbow him in the ribs and then turn and jam his eyes with two fingers.

Then Nancy went into action and grabbed the gun and whirled to a standing position, a bloody spot on her left temple. "Let go of my daughter, you idiot."

Emma rushed forward and kicked the gun from the man, who now stood with watering eyes, her hard boot tip hitting his hand. And just for good measure, she stomped her boot hard against his shin and then flipped him to the floor.

He screamed in wrath just as the back door burst open and Ryder rushed in, his head bleeding.

Ryder advanced, shouting at the man, "Don't move."

But he stopped when he found his mother and Emma holding a gun on the stranger and Stephanie wrapping his hands with duct tape.

While Emma held her booted foot against his spine.

"You can't hold me here," the man said after Ryder had practically dragged him out to the barn.

"Yes, I can," Ryder retorted, his mind on the three women he'd left in the kitchen, his head throbbing from being hit from behind.

He'd been hit but he'd managed to get up and take down the man who'd rammed his head with a handgun. That man had gone down with one punch, but he was now missing. He'd gotten up and run away from what they could tell.

Nancy had a gash on her head and his sister had been

terrified, but thanks to Emma, they were both alive and well. The intruder had used a tranquilizer dart on Spur but the big dog was slowly coming awake. They'd found him outside underneath some trees.

"You tried to harm my family, and since I'm an officer of the law, I can hold you here all night if I decide to do that. You know, we have our own law this far from the city."

"He's messing with me, ain't he?" the nervous man asked the local sheriff. "Ain't I supposed to be taken to jail or something?"

"Or something," said the sheriff, one year from retirement and not happy about being interrupted during his supper. "I'm tired of having to ride out here, so I might just let Detective Palladin take care of you, know what I mean?"

"I was only following orders."

"From who?" Ryder said, leaning in, the anger he'd held in check boiling over. "And don't lie to me. I'm not in the mood, got it?"

The sheriff paced around. "Start by telling us your name."

"Don't I get a lawyer?"

Ryder lifted the man by his dirty shirt collar. "You'll get a lot more than that if you don't answer some questions. Your partner ran off and left you, so it would be to your benefit if you start talking."

"Dexter," the man said, his eyes bulging. "Dexter Kerry. Look, they told me to get in here and grab the woman. Only I found two women so I grabbed the younger one. But the old one swung at me with a frying pan, so I hit her with my gun, then grabbed the screaming one."

Ryder slammed the man back down into the old chair. "Those two women are my mother and my sister, so you can understand why I'm so upset, right?"

"Well, I need the other one."

"You mean the redhead?"

The man bobbed his head. "She's hard to pin down."

Ryder knew that only too well, but for once he was glad Emma hadn't listened to him. If she had gone to the cabin, his mom and sister could have both been killed and someone could have gone after her, too.

"So you're admitting that you came here to find this redheaded woman and take her? Kill her? What exactly?"

"The big man gave Mickey and me a wad of cash up front and promised more later. Wanted us to bring her to him, personally. So we waited for y'all to show up. Me inside and Mickey out back."

"Who is the big man?"

"I can't tell you that. He'll kill me."

"If you don't tell me that, you'll go to prison for attempted kidnapping and murder…and someone will kill you there. Work with me here," Ryder said, "and we might be able to cut a deal."

"It'll have to be a big deal," the man responded, his fear apparent.

"Prison is a very big deal," the sheriff chimed in. "Attempted kidnapping and murder are two very big deals. And your friend Mickey is long gone by now, but my men are right behind him. They'll get him to talk."

"I ain't talking and I'll need to see a lawyer."

Ryder could only guess who that lawyer would be, too. "Do you know Brian Purdue?"

The man turned green. "Nope."

"Yes, I'm thinking," Ryder replied. "We have Brian at the downtown station. He's talking a lot. You need to tell us who sent you here."

Dexter swallowed. "What kind of deal can I get?"

"You get to live for starters," Ryder said.

"Manchester," Dexter spit out. "B. D. Manchester."

"As in Bobby Doug Manchester?" Ryder asked, his heart beating a heavy cadence.

"The one and only," Dexter said. "I'll need protection from him. He has people everywhere."

"Name some of them."

"His mistress works for the Wood Hills substation. Rhonda Harper."

His mistress? It all made sense to Ryder now.

Ryder shot Sheriff Watson a grim glance. "Sheriff, I'm gonna have to take him in to the station for more questioning and so he can give us a solid confession and statement with his lawyer present."

When Dexter scoffed, Ryder added, "And to protect him until we can figure out what to do with him."

Dexter turned green with fear, but he nodded and settled down. "I'm caught between a rock and a hard place," he said on a defeated tone.

"I reckon you are," the sheriff said with a tired-of-this tone. "Have at it, Palladin. I'll even loan you a deputy to get him there so you can get on with finding that girl."

"I'd appreciate that," Ryder said. "If you don't mind loading him in while I go to the house to check on my family, I'd appreciate it." He motioned to two of his men to help, just in case.

"Before you go, where is Manchester?" Ryder asked, anger boiling hot in his system.

"He's waiting in the basement at the Triple B. We're supposed to bring Emma Langston there."

Ryder lifted Dexter up again. "And where is the girl, Reese Parker?"

"I don't know about any girl."

TWENTY-ONE

Ryder hurried to tell Emma what he'd found. She'd want in on this, and after everything she'd done to protect not only herself but him and his family, too, she deserved to be in the thick now that things were finally falling into place.

When he got to the house, he found his mother and sister making sandwiches. But no Emma.

"What's going on?" he asked, concern threading through his veins.

His mother glanced around. "We thought y'all would be hungry. Didn't Emma come and find you?"

"Emma. I haven't seen her."

"She went out a couple minutes ago," Stephanie said. "Headed to the barn to find you."

Ryder's heart did a little stomp. "I haven't seen her."

Then he heard a vehicle revving to life.

"I've got to go," he said, hurrying out the back door.

She'd taken one of the ranch vehicles. He saw the taillights heading up the long driveway. Calling Pierce, he shouted, "I think Emma overheard our intruder talking and now she's on her way to the Triple B to confront Bobby Doug Manchester. Be aware and stop her. I'm right behind her."

Ryder called her cell. She didn't pick up. He left a message. "Emma, don't do this. We can go in together. He's a dangerous man. Don't do this."

He caught up with her on the interstate, but she zig-zagged and sped up, trying to lose him. Ryder prayed she'd come to her senses. She had to have heard most of the interrogation and now she was out for vigilante justice.

Ryder hit the gas and tried to catch her, all the reasons he needed to stay away from her moving past him like the signs on the road. But only one thing stayed with him.

He was in love with her, and now his worst fears were coming to light. He'd fought against love for too long. If he had the chance, he'd tell her that.

He only prayed he'd get to her in time.

Emma parked a block away and made it to the bar. She took in air and told herself to be more like Ryder. To stay calm and rational and think her way through the waves of emotions overtaking her body.

"You want me, Manchester? Well, here I come," Emma whispered, thinking if the man thought he could get away with this, he was sorely wrong.

Checking the gun Ryder had given her earlier, she gathered her thoughts and shook off the creeping panic. She had to stay strong for Reese's sake. And for Ryder. If she got herself shot, he'd never forgive her.

He'd never forgive her anyway for sneaking out like this, but the minute she'd heard that Bobby Doug was the man in charge and that he was waiting for them to bring her to him, Emma knew what she had to do.

Confront the man who took her daughter.

Emma hit the sidewalk, her boots clicking away, and suddenly she remembered everything about that night when she'd done this very thing just a week or so ago.

She hadn't panicked that night. She'd been full of self-righteous rage and daring.

She'd be more aware now, though.

Ryder had taught her that. He was good at his job because he was cautious and calculating and thorough. He had to be to stay alive. She'd be careful, but she would find Reese before the night was over.

The bar wasn't that busy, so she stood in the shadows by the old front door and took in the place. A few rough-looking men at the main bar and two women sitting at a back table.

Emma studied the women, one older and worn, burned out. The other young and pretty…and scared.

Tessa Clark.

The two women glanced up. Tessa's eyes went wide, but she didn't say or do anything. She looked from Emma to the door off to the side of the bar. The door that led to the basement.

Emma gave her a slight nod, her gut telling her the girl wouldn't rat her out.

A couple of the men at the bar got up and hurried after her. "Hey, lady, you can't go down there."

Emma whirled and gave them her brightest smile. "I need to speak to Bobby Doug Manchester. He's expecting me."

The two men backed off. Emma eased the gun out from underneath her shirt. She didn't bother knocking. Whirling through the door, she drew her gun and stared down the surprised face of the man who'd tried to kill her. Several times.

He jumped up, his hands in the air, his dark hair slick with gel. "Well, well," he said, laughing in her face. "Remind me to hire you. You are one tenacious woman."

"You have no idea."

She slammed the door with her boot and then advanced. "Why don't you make this easy and take me to the girl?"

"I don't know what you're talking about. I only wanted to find you so you'd stop harassing everyone. No one knows where that girl is. She ran away."

"Purdue didn't say that," she teased, daring him to blink.

"I don't know any Purdue."

"Your lawyer does."

"You mean this lawyer?" He motioned behind her.

Emma whirled to find John Clayton sitting in a chair in the corner. And he had a gun aimed at her.

"Yeah, he's the one," she said, not ready to give up just yet.

Ryder burst through the front door but found the seedy, dull bar nearly empty. Ignoring the men walking toward him, he headed down to the basement and saw that the office door was open. No one was inside the office, and the door leading up to the alley lay back against it hinges.

"Stop," he heard a man behind him shout.

Ryder turned and held up his badge and his gun. "Dallas police. Where did they go?"

The man held up his hands, palms out. "I don't ask questions, man."

"Then get lost."

Ryder took off up the stairs to the street just in time to see a sleek black BMW peeling out of the parking lot. Where was Pierce?

His earbud crackled. "Ryder, we got people here, but they took her. They had a gun to her head and…we had to let 'em go."

"Which way?"

"East. We're tailing one car now."

Ryder ran to his truck and got in. "They took two cars?"

"Yes. I'm following a gray sportscar."

"Sam Pittman. I'll track the BMW."

Ryder cranked and peeled away, but a woman came running out of the shadows just past the alley, causing him to slam on brakes.

"Emma?"

No. Tessa Clark. The girl banged on the door and he reached over and opened it, his gun trained on her. "What?"

"He's taking her to a rental about fifteen miles from here near the Trinity River." She named the address.

"Tessa, do they have Reese somewhere?"

"Yes."

"Do you need help?"

"Yes. And I can help you."

Ryder motioned. "Get in."

The girl did as he asked, looking behind her. "I slugged that woman who had me and I ran out the front door and hid. I saw Manchester put her in the BMW. The others scattered, too afraid of the cops now to come after me."

Sirens sounded in the distance. "And right on time," Ryder replied.

Ryder let Pierce know he had Tessa Clark and was in pursuit of Bobby Doug Manchester. Now he could only pray that they got to him in time to save both Emma and Reese.

Emma glared at the man forcing her to drive his car. "Just tell me. Is Reese alive?"

"You'll never know," Bobby Doug said, his gun glinting in the moonlight. "You just couldn't leave well enough alone."

"Kidnapping a teenaged girl is not *well enough*. That's

a crime. A felony. Hard time. But then, this is just one of many, right?"

"Shut up and drive. You won't be around to find that out either."

Emma tried to convince him. "I don't care what you do with me, but let Reese go."

"Can't do that, sweetheart. She's become an annoyance, and my wife doesn't like annoying people."

His wife was in on this?

Emma had to think. They were on a long, winding road that followed hills and bluffs. If she could swerve the car in just the right direction, she might be able to escape and call for help. But then, she had to find out where they were holding Reese.

"Where are we going?"

"You ask too many questions."

"You said I was good at my job."

"Too good and now you've got that pretty boy Ryder Palladin hounding my people, too. Has to end."

"It will," Emma promised him. "One way or another."

"Too bad about this," Bobby Doug said, his hand slipping down her cheek like a snake about to attack. "I like a woman who puts up a good fight."

Emma held back the bile in her throat and prayed this man had not hurt Reese. She also prayed that even if she died tonight, he'd be brought to justice. Then she saw her chance. A big curve ahead and…a guard rail near what looked like a drop-off below. Emma hit the gas, causing the man beside her to shift in his seat, fear filling his eyes.

They caught up with Bobby Doug's car in a matter of minutes since Ryder had doubled down on the gas pedal.

"Is this where they were going to take you the other night?" he asked, trying to get the girl to open up.

"Yes, but when they saw someone following us they changed directions."

"When we caused the crash, you ran away?"

Tessa lowered her head. "Yes, but they caught me."

The BMW sped up and took off along a big curve in the road. Ryder sped behind the car, staying on the sleek sedan.

"Ryder, look out," Tessa said, grabbing the dash.

The car ahead swerved to the left and overcorrected. Ryder watched in horror as the car smashed into a guard rail, crashing and then bouncing back on the road. For a minute, he thought the car would roll back over the crashed rail, but it came to a rolling stop, tittering against the unstable railing.

Ryder slammed on his brakes and got out of the truck.

"Stay here," he told Tessa. Then he opened the glove compartment and handed her a pistol. "Just in case."

The girl was crying, but she nodded her head.

Ryder ran toward the crash site, watching in horror as the passenger-side door swung open. Bobby Doug Manchester crawled out, screaming as he tried to stand, blood coming out of his chest, a gun dangling in his right hand. He dropped the gun and fell to the ground.

Ignoring him, Ryder called, "Emma?"

The driver's side door opened and Emma stumbled out. Ryder ran to her and took her into his arms. "Emma, are you all right?"

She nodded and held her head. "Is he dead?"

"Ryder!"

Ryder heard Tessa's scream and saw Bobby Doug clawing, his fingers gripping the gun he'd dropped. Ryder whirled toward the injured man, his own weapon raised. "Stop, Bobby Doug."

The other man seemed caught between a sob and a

laugh, his hand shaking, the gun wobbling as he tried to aim. "Can't do that. Ruin everything."

Ryder kept walking until he stood gun-to-gun with Bobby Doug. "Tell us where Reese Parker is."

"Can't." Bobby Doug moved an inch closer, his gun drawn. "Can't. Too late."

Rising toward Ryder, he lifted the gun.

A shot rang out over the night, followed by another.

Bobby Doug fell to the ground, moaning.

Ryder whirled. "Emma?" She was gone.

"We're here."

Tessa had gotten out of the truck and Emma stood holding the girl around her waist. Tessa held the gun Ryder had given her.

"She shot but missed," Emma said. "She's okay."

Emma and Ryder rushed toward the man on the ground. Bobby Doug gasped for air.

"Where is Reese Parker?" Emma asked.

Bobby Doug shook his head, his eyes full of sadness.

"Sabrina," he said, grabbing Emma's hand. "Sabrina."

Then his eyes went cold and he stopped breathing.

TWENTY-TWO

"We need to get to that cabin," Emma said, her eyes on the dead man at her feet.

Ryder nodded. "Get Tessa back in the truck." Then he called in the wreck and the shooting. He'd give a full report later.

Ryder pushed the pickup around curves and ravines, holding the road until they turned off on a bumpy dirt lane leading to an isolated lot near the river.

"Emma, you could have been killed. What were you thinking?"

"You know what I was thinking," she retorted, her chest and head sore from the air bag. "I had to do something. So I crashed the car, grabbed his gun and helped him shoot himself. You finished him off."

Ryder's eyes went wide. "You are one dangerous woman."

"This is it," Tessa said, breaking the stare-down between them. "Park here."

Ryder pulled off the lane and they walked the rest of the way. "Tessa, you stay behind us and out of sight. If something happens, run back to the truck and call for help. Understand?"

Tessa nodded. "They held me here once."

Emma's heart hammered in fits of joy and rage. She only prayed that Reese was inside the cabin and alive. Each step sounded into the night, making her cringe with fear and determination.

Ryder moved ahead, both of them crouching in the shadows while Tessa hid behind a giant tree.

When they reached the cabin, Ryder pulled Emma close underneath a window. Together, they slowly lifted up enough to see inside.

Emma gasped, causing Ryder to put a finger to her lips.

Reese sat tied up in a straight chair while a slender woman with upswept blond hair paced in front of her.

The woman halted in front of Reese. "As soon as Bobby Doug gets here, we are ending this. You'll either be dead or a long way from Texas, little girl. It's your fault we've had to go to such extreme measures. You just wouldn't leave us alone."

Reese glared up at the well-dressed Sabrina Manchester. "I told you, your husband threatened to kill me when I heard him talking about a drug shipment. He threatened me and my family, and you had poor Tessa spying on me. We moved away. I haven't told a soul."

"But you threatened to tell the world," Sabrina shouted. "And then you disappeared. We had to search the whole state of Texas. But Sarabeth found a picture of you with that sniveling Tessa online. She hates both of you, but she loves her daddy and me. So she told us where you and your overprotective parents had moved. We found you. You won't snitch on us, ever."

Sabrina turned away as if she'd heard something. "That must be Bobby Doug now. He's held you here long enough. He doesn't have the strength to kill you, so we'll just let our men send you far away."

Emma shifted, the need to save her daughter washing over her in waves of rage and fear. Emma lifted her head another inch, hoping Reese would see her there in the moonlight. Reese looked her way. Emma gave Reese a thumbs-up signal. When Sabrina whirled around, Reese started crying and twitching.

"Stop it! Your tears don't move me, honey."

Shaking her head, her long tangled hair flying out, Reese began to put up a real fight. "You need to let me go. I'm telling you, you really should."

Sabrina slapped Reese. "I'm gonna keep you alive but far away. You'll suffer more that way."

Emma stood. "I'm going in."

Ryder whispered, "I'm right behind you."

With that, Emma used her booted foot to kick open the rickety old door, her gun aimed at Sabrina Manchester.

Sabrina whirled, a hand to her heart. "Who are you and where's Bobby Doug?"

"I'm Emma Langston," Emma said. "Bobby Doug won't be joining us. He's lying dead a few miles up the road."

Sabrina's heavily made-up face crumbled. "What? What are you talking about?"

Ryder grabbed her hands and cuffed her while Emma held a gun on her. Then he told her who he was and why he was here. "It's over, Mrs. Manchester. Bobby Doug gave us your name before he died, and right now, the Triple B is being taken over by the Dallas police. Two of your men are in jail, and they're singing your praises to beat the band."

Sabrina let out a wail, tears smearing her mascara. "No. No. Let me go. This isn't right."

"It's not only right, it's the law." Ryder guided her toward the door. When she saw Tessa, she spat at her. "We should have killed both of you."

"Tessa!" Reese started crying again. "Tessa, they told me you were dead."

Tessa ran to where Emma hurriedly kneeled and untied Reese. Emma sat back, holding back tears of relief. "Are you okay, Reese?"

"I have a cold and I need a shower and some food," Reese said. "I prayed someone would find me."

"You're safe now," Emma said, helping Reese out of the chair. "We'll get you home…to your parents."

Ryder met her gaze, admiration in his eyes. Along with acceptance and resolve.

She wanted to say something to him, but Reese fell against her. "I don't know who you are, but thank you for saving my life."

Emma nodded. "You're welcome."

Then Tessa and Emma hugged each other tight.

"Sarabeth pretended to be my friend after you moved away," Tessa said. "But she wanted to get to you. She hates you. They told her lies about both of us. I'm so sorry I fell for her tricks. They are horrible, evil people."

Emma would hear the rest of Tessa's story later. Right now, she just wanted to get Reese home where she belonged. It would be one of the hardest things she'd ever had to do, but Reese was alive. And Emma would sacrifice anything for that.

Three days later

Emma stared up at the massive door to the Parkers' mansion, her palms sweaty and her heart pushing her into what could become a panic attack.

But the strong hand holding hers squeezed tight when she rang the doorbell. "You sure about this?"

She looked over at Ryder. "I think so. I'll let Reese decide if she wants me in her life. But at least I can leave here knowing she's okay. That's all I ever wanted."

Ryder gave her one of those intense stares she'd come to know. Now that they'd cracked the case and Sabrina Manchester and her gang had been rounded up and put in jail, they'd both taken a day to get their heads together. Now they seemed to be doing that dance again. The one where they circled around each other.

She still didn't know if Ryder wanted her in his life. She'd been reckless and impulsive, but her daughter was alive. Should she be happy with that and go on with her life? He'd indicated she was free to go. Free to do whatever she wanted.

She wanted *him* but first…

The door opened and Annette Parker held out her arms to Emma. "Come in, please."

Emma hugged her close, her emotions rolling and tumbling like sagebrush. "How is she?"

Annette glanced out to the sunroom. "She's good. Quiet but healing. The doctors gave her the all clear, but she'll take it easy the rest of the summer and go through therapy for the trauma."

"Are you sure I won't add to that trauma?"

"I think she could use the truth right now," Annette said. "She's always known she was adopted and she's been curious. So you're already *our* hero. Why not become her friend, too?"

Joseph came into the hallway and hugged Emma, then shook Reese's hand. "She's waiting."

Ryder gave Emma one last glance. "I'll be with the Parkers."

"We'd love to show you the garden," Annette said.

Emma watched them walk toward the kitchen door and then took a deep breath. The panic attack she'd expected didn't come. Instead a sense of peace and closure came over her. She walked into the wide, sunny room where Reese sat with a tabby cat and smiled down at the girl.

"Hi, Reese."

"Hi, Emma." Reese got up and held the cat close. "This is Goldie. He's a big spoiled baby."

Emma took the purring cat and smiled. "I had a cat once when I was growing up, but I moved around a lot and I had to leave him behind."

"I guess that made you sad," Reese said.

Emma didn't want to think about her old memories anymore. "Yes, but life does that sometimes. How are you?"

"I'm okay," Reese said. "Mom said you wanted to talk to me."

Emma gave Goldie back to her and nodded. "Yes."

Reese let the cat go, and he took off to the far side of the room. "Do you need more information on what happened?"

"No, we've got your statement and Tessa has been very helpful. They apparently took her a few days ago and she tried to escape when we tailed them, but they found her and brought her back to the Triple B the other night."

"They planned to kill both of us," Reese said. "But then you and Ryder came along."

"Thankfully."

"I am thankful," Reese said. Then she tossed her auburn hair. "And I think I know why you're here."

"You do."

"Yes." She motioned to an antique mirror over a rattan settee. Then she took Emma's hand. "Look at us."

Emma stared into the mirror and realized she was also

staring at a mirror image. Her throat burning with emotions, she said, "We are sure a pair."

Reese's eyes welled with tears. "Yes, we are. As if we were sisters…or maybe mother and daughter?"

The hope in that question stunned Emma. "We could be mother and daughter. That is, if you want your birth mother in your life."

Reese gulped a sob and turned and fell into Emma's arms. "Are you kidding? You saved my life and…you're beautiful and I know you sacrificed a lot to give me this life and I love my parents but…can we stay friends? Can I get to know you?"

"Yes, yes, yes." Emma cried against the strawberry scent of her daughter's hair. "Oh, yes. What would you like to do first?"

Reese stood back and wiped at her tears. "I'd love a good cheeseburger."

Emma stared out at the nervous man in the garden with Emma's equally nervous parents. "I think that can be arranged."

Two days later, Ryder stood on the cabin porch waiting. Would she show?

Or had she left town already?

The case was a wrap. All the DNA evidence from the Triple B alley and from the cup Emma had found on the road matched up—Bobby Doug had been there that night and Reese had been brought there by Brian Purdue. They'd impounded Brian Purdue's truck and found Reese's fingerprints on the door and the dash and strands of her hair on the seat. Tessa Clark had given a statement and was now seeking therapy and counseling. Bounce and Ounce had been located and taken into custody. All of the Manchesters' minions had become very chatty about the whole operation.

"You should tell her how you feel," Stephanie had suggested in a firm tone at breakfast.

"And how do you think I feel, Oh-Great-And-Knowing-One?"

"You're in love with Emma," his mother had shouted before Stephanie could retort. "Buy that woman a burger and tell her you want to spend the rest of your life with her."

So he'd invited Emma and Reese out to the ranch and he'd ordered up a six-pack of his favorite burgers. With the works.

Now he waited. And waited. Spur waited with him, the dog's ear perking up with each sound or movement.

After thirty-five excruciating minutes, he looked toward the big house and saw Emma and Reese walking toward him, his mother and sister chattering away with who-knew-what kind of advice. Spur danced and ran in a confused pattern all around them.

Emma wore a dress. A dress? A bright, floral, flowing dress, her hair down around her shoulders and…a new pair of boots. Buttered tan.

The lively foursome stopped at the pond and Reese waved to him. He started that way, but Emma moved toward him first. Spur decided he'd follow Emma, of course.

While the other three held back and suddenly became deeply involved in studying the water.

She strolled through the grass with purpose and intent.

Good. He had some purpose and intent stored up, too. He had a good mind to tell her off about that stunt she'd pulled. But then, a sweet floral scent assaulted him and he figured he could live with her boldness as long as he could inhale that beautiful flower garden for the rest of his life.

"What's it gonna be, cowboy?" Emma asked, her eyes going green in a deep forest mode.

"What do you mean, PI Langston?"

"I mean, Detective Palladin, do you want me to stay? Can you handle me in your life? Or…are you still stuck in that tired excuse about your work and how women don't get it?"

Ryder thought he'd feel the same old fear, that dread of bringing a woman into his world. But today, he felt light and free and happy. Really happy.

So he came down the steps and scooped her close. "I want you to stay. I can handle you in my life. And I'm not stuck in that excuse about my work anymore. In fact, I'm thinking I might like to work with the sheriff's department. You know, a little closer to home."

"That sounds good," Emma said. "Then you'll have a life, right?"

"Yes. I'll come home to you every night."

"And I can still do my job until…until you can come home to me and…our children."

"We're gonna have children?"

"Lots of 'em," she said, tears misty against her grin.

Ryder ran a hand through her hair. "Does that mean you'll marry me?"

She nodded, her eyes holding his. "Yes, and that means all of my panic is in the past and I'm going to make new memories here with you. Good memories. No more undercover memories."

"Well, maybe a few," he whispered against her ear.

Then he kissed her and lifted her up into his arms. "I love you."

"I love you, too. We can run from danger, but it's sure hard to run away from love." She smiled and then she said, "Do I smell cheeseburgers?"

The trio behind them clapped and came running. Spur barked his approval and ran around in circles.

And then, they had a picnic in the yard by the water.

Emma Langston had a family to love at last.

And the vice squad cowboy had come out of the shadows.

* * * * *

Dear Reader,

I love setting stories in Texas. It's a big, vast place with a million stories to tell. This one grabbed me and I had to write it. Emma made the ultimate sacrifice, and then she had to make another sacrifice after temporarily losing her memory. But her fears kept her from doing what she needed to do.

Ryder was on a quest for justice, thinking if he caught enough bad guys he could appease his father's tragic and senseless death. This story is about doing the right thing for all the wrong reasons and about sacrificing what could have been for what needed to be.

Together, these two tormented characters came together one dark night and decided to find the truth by helping each other. Sometimes, it seems we are plunged into darkness and that God does not hear our pleas. But He leaves signs along the way to guide us. Like Ryder and Emma, we have to listen, search and be open to those signs. They both found the justice they were seeking, and their sacrifices finally paid off.

I hope you look for the light at the end of the darkness and watch for the signs that the Lord sends. I hope you enjoyed going on this quest with Emma and Ryder. And if you've never been to Texas, then what are you waiting for?

Until next time, may the angels watch over you. Always.

Lenora Worth

COMING NEXT MONTH FROM
Love Inspired® Suspense

Available November 6, 2018

VALIANT DEFENDER
Military K-9 Unit • by Shirlee McCoy

When Captain Justin Blackwood's teenage daughter is kidnapped by the serial killer he's been hunting, he's desperate to stop the Red Rose Killer from making her his next victim. Can he and Captain Gretchen Hill and their K-9 partners save his daughter and capture a killer?

AMISH CHRISTMAS EMERGENCY
Amish Country Justice • by Dana R. Lynn

Alexa Grant's stalker is determined that if he can't have her, nobody can—even if it means killing her. And as she searches for a safe haven in Amish country, it's Sergeant Gavin Jackson's job to protect Alexa...or risk losing her to a deadly secret admirer.

LOST CHRISTMAS MEMORIES
Gold Country Cowboys • by Dana Mentink

Tracy Wilson witnessed a murder—but after a head injury, she can't remember who it was. Now someone plans to silence her for good, and only cowboy Keegan Thorn believes her. Can she recover her memory in time to save her life?

CHRISTMAS HIDEOUT
McKade Law • by Susan Sleeman

Fleeing from her dangerous ex-boyfriend, single mother Nicole Dyer takes refuge in a cabin on a ranch—and is discovered by the owner, Deputy Matt McKade. When threats escalate to attempts on Nicole's life, Matt is the only one she trusts to keep her and her daughter safe.

DEADLY CHRISTMAS DUTY
Covert Operatives • by Virginia Vaughan

Former navy SEAL Noah Cason turns to prosecutor Melinda Steele for help getting justice for his sister. But when Melinda is attacked, she and her son are the ones who need *his* help. Under Noah's protection, can they stay alive long enough to figure out who wants them dead?

CHRISTMAS UNDER FIRE
Mountie Brotherhood • by Michelle Karl

It's Mountie Aaron Thrace's duty to guard visiting dignitary Cally Roslin during her stay in Canada—but he never expects he'll be facing down ruthless assailants determined that she won't survive the holidays. With danger and a snowstorm closing in, can he make sure she lives to see Christmas?

LISCNM1018

SPECIAL EXCERPT FROM

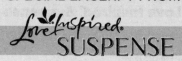

Love Inspired.
SUSPENSE

*The final battle with the Red Rose Killer begins when he
kidnaps Captain Justin Blackwood's teenage daughter.*

Read on for a sneak preview of
Valiant Defender *by Shirlee McCoy,*
the exciting conclusion to the Military K-9 Unit miniseries,
available November 2018 from Love Inspired Suspense.

Canyon Air Force Base was silent. Houses shuttered,
lights off. Streets quiet. Just the way it should be in the
darkest hours of the morning. Captain Justin Blackwood
didn't let the quiet make him complacent. Seven months
ago, an enemy had infiltrated the base. Boyd Sullivan, aka
the Red Rose Killer—a man who'd murdered five people
in his hometown before he'd been caught—had escaped
from prison and continued his crime spree, murdering
several more people and wreaking havoc on the base.

"What are your thoughts, Captain?" Captain Gretchen
Hill asked as he sped through the quiet community.

"I don't think we're going to find him at the house," he
responded. "But when it comes to Boyd Sullivan, I believe
in checking out every lead."

"The witness reported lights? She didn't actually see
Boyd?"

"She didn't see him, but the family who lived in the
house left for a new post two days ago. Lots of moving

trucks and activity. She's worried Sullivan might have noticed and decided to squat in the empty property."

"Based on how easily Boyd has slipped through our fingers these past few months, I'd say he's too smart to squat in base housing," Gretchen said.

"I agree," Justin responded. He'd been surprised at how much he enjoyed working with Gretchen. He'd expected her presence to feel like a burden, one more person to worry about and protect. But she had razor-sharp intellect and a calm, focused demeanor that had been an asset to the team.

"Even if he decided to spend a few nights in an empty house, why turn on lights?"

"If he's there, he wants us to know it," Justin responded. It was the only explanation that made sense. And it was the kind of game Sullivan liked to play—taunting his intended victims, letting them know that he was closing in.

He needed to be stopped.

Tonight.

For the sake of the people on base and for his daughter Portia's sake.

Don't miss
Valiant Defender *by Shirlee McCoy,*
available November 2018 wherever
Love Inspired® Suspense books and ebooks are sold.

www.LoveInspired.com

Get 4 FREE REWARDS!

We'll send you 2 FREE Books plus 2 FREE Mystery Gifts.

Love Inspired® Suspense books feature Christian characters facing challenges to their faith... and lives.

FREE
Value Over
$20
